THE WILD HUNTSBOYS

THE WILD HUNTSBOYS

MARTIN STEWART

VIKING

VIKING

An imprint of Penguin Random House LLC, New York

First published in the United States of America by Viking,
an imprint of Penguin Random House, LLC, 2021.

Visit us online at penguinrandomhouse.com

Library of Congress Cataloging-in-Publication Data is available.

Printed in Canada

ISBN 9780593116135

1 3 5 7 9 10 8 6 4 2

Design by Opal Roengchai.
Text set in Bohemia LT Std.

For Julie

Up the airy mountain,
Down the rushy glen,
We daren't go a-hunting
For fear of little men.

The Fairies, William Allingham

No rain but thunder, and the sound of giants.

Hellboy: The Wild Hunt, Mike Mignola

PART ONE

1

The faerie folk are glad to help
They're glad to lend a hand
They'll keep the milk and shine the silk
They're noble and they're grand!
They'll gladly churn your butter
Or they'll polish up the wood
They'll even buff the silver
Oh! They really are so good!

Traditional song, anonymous

"How do you make a plane out of a frying pan?" said Elena, leaping onto the pavement.

Luka caught up to her, gripping Hugo's collar.

"You melt it down," he said, "then when it's all runny you turn it into something else: plane, tank, bomb. Whatever."

"What about the handle?"

Luka brushed at his jacket. It was thick with demolition dust—just like the rest of him. There had been more raids in the last week, and the fog of broken bricks was everywhere.

He checked his phone, then dropped it in his pocket as an army jeep buzzed past.

"What?" he said.

Elena wrinkled her nose. "Like, our frying pan's got a plastic handle, so—"

"God, Ellie, I don't know. The Government's run out of metal, so they're taking ours, all right?"

They looked at the trucks that lined North Street—their deep, clattering bellies piled high with pots, pans, spoons, knives, benches, bathtubs, and bikes. There were even radiators, sticking out of the heaps like broken teeth.

"It's scary," said Elena.

Luka shrugged. "It's just stuff."

But his sister shook her head, bouncing her dark ponytail against his elbow. "It's not," she said. "It's people. People lived with these things and painted them and . . . hung their pants on them! Imagine if we—"

A City Warden stepped into the road, the winter sun shining white behind his square helmet.

Elena shuffled under Luka's arm while Hugo growled, deep in his chest.

The Warden banged a passing truck's flank like he was spurring a horse. As the thing rumbled off in a clank of dust and fumes, they saw the bomb-damaged house it had emptied out gaping like a ribcage: stairs leading nowhere, pictures hung on half walls, hallways like torn throats.

Luka shivered.

"I wonder what the Islands will be like," said Elena,

lowering her voice and watching the Wardens crawl
through the guts of the ruined home.

"Quiet," said Luka, grabbing his jeans to pull his
weak leg onto the pavement. "They don't get bombing
raids. There's no army there. It'll be quiet."

"I hope there's rabbits and deer and things."

"It's the countryside."

"So?"

"So of *course* there are. What do you think you're
going to eat?"

She hit his arm. "I never would."

Hugo stopped to sniff a lamppost, then cocked his
leg.

"You will if you get hungry enough," Luka said over
the rattle of dog pee. "You promised Mum. You need
to eat, even if—"

"I know. But there'll be enough veggies for me. I'm
only little—and they must have powdered avocado
and things."

Luka shuddered.

"Even real avocado was yuk. It was green. You
won't remember."

They walked a moment in silence, footsteps shadowed by the rasp of Luka's dragging foot.

"I wish you could come with me," Elena said.

Luka bit the inside of his lip.

"I know. But I'm too old—ten was the cutoff. I
missed it by miles."

"By a year."

"You'll be fine. You're *always* fine."

"I hope so," said Elena softly.

Luka touched the top of her head, then checked his phone.

"I'm out of minutes—how long till the train leaves?"

"You *always* use your ration straightaway," said Elena, her eyebrow curving in a way that reminded Luka of their mother.

"I know, but I can't get used to it. Or the curfew. I mean, switching off data *and* Wi-Fi at sundown. It's not fair."

"You never know who's listening," said Elena, imitating the voice from the advert as she checked her own phone. "It's fine," she said, "we've got four minutes, so we don't need to—"

"*Four?* We need to run—come on!"

He pushed her gas mask and bag into her hands and ran unevenly behind her into the old town, slipping on the slobber of a window-cleaner's wash as he landed on the cobbles.

"Luka!" shouted Elena, turning to wait for him as Hugo barked and ran in circles. "Come on!"

"No, *you* keep going!" said Luka, scrambling to his feet. "You can't miss it!"

They ran toward the clock tower, Hugo bounding ahead as they weaved through greasy food stalls and sign-waving protestors, between cables pooled behind the pop-up barracks and finally—gasping so much the air felt like thumbs pressing into their windpipes— down the train station's big, wide steps.

Elena stopped so suddenly Luka ran into her.

"Ow!" he said. "Why did you—"

Central Station was a hive of neat soldiers and nervous children, their energies swirling under the glass roof in a shrill, piano-wire pitch.

He took his sister's hand.

"You're on platform nine," he said stiffly.

She nodded, and they moved into the throng.

All the parents had been called up to fight or pressed into service, so the farewells had fallen to the older children, who—prematurely aged by the War's strange freedoms and responsibilities—had become a colony of miniature grown-ups in the City's great hive. Government flags hung from the old clock, ration posters plastered the chicory coffee shop, and a thousand children cried and stared and babbled into phones, bug-eyed gas masks hanging around their necks.

They stood under the vast departures board, bathing in the pale light of distant places: the Highlands, Islands, and Lakesides to which they were being sent, as far from Bellum City's bomb-stinking chaos as could be imagined.

An official War Effort message pushed the timetables aside on the board: BE CAREFUL WITH THE POSTS YOU MAKE—YOUR FAMILY'S FATE COULD BE AT STAKE. Luka felt his pocket buzz with the matching text as they pushed toward Elena's platform.

He wanted to say something, to say *everything*, but his thoughts were too hot and too fast and the words stuck in his neck in a solid, painful lump.

"Ellie," he managed, as they arrived at Elena's platform. "I wanted to—"

"You need to promise me something," she cut him off, glancing over her shoulder.

"Anything, of course, I—"

"You need to feed the faeries when I'm gone."

Luka closed his eyes. "We've talked about this. You're *eight*, it's time you—"

"I'm *not* making it up!" Ellie whispered, grabbing his arm. "You do magic too, so—"

"Mine's not magic," said Luka. He pressed his coin into the palm of his right hand, then appeared it from behind her ear. "They're tricks. I make them happen. If I could do real magic, I'd stop the War and you could stay."

Elena let out a single sob, but wiped her cheeks and pulled him close.

"Feeding the faeries is the same thing! My offering makes the magic happen—and they get so *angry* if they don't get their food."

"Maybe it's different now there's a war on."

She shook her head. "They don't care what's happening in our world, they just want food. You have to feed them—you *have* to. Promise me!"

"Ellie, I don't—" Luka pulled at his hair.

"Promise!" she hissed.

Luka opened his mouth to protest—then he saw the look in her eyes. "All right," he said. "I will. If it makes you happy."

She gave him a quick, strong hug.

"Tonight, then," she whispered, bending to scratch Hugo's ears. "Put a bowl of bread and milk outside my window." She threw her arms around him. "I love you."

"Ellie," he said, blinking away the light-headedness that tingled up from his feet.

Elena pushed through the barrier, where a Warden held a scanner under her thumb.

As she boarded the train, the screen above Luka flashed bright red, and he gripped his coin so tightly that he gasped with the pain. In a few seconds the world had changed: he'd become a boy whose sister had been evacuated, whose family was incomplete—a boy the War had begun to squeeze with all its might.

Elena was gone. He would walk back through the City alone.

Luka felt the first prickle of the realization that she

really *was* being taken away, that he would not see her or hear her voice.

What if he never saw her again?

Elena turned from the top step. Her skin was olive, like his; her hair dark and straight, like his; and she seemed, to Luka, to be as perfect and small as she had ever been.

She looked at him and mouthed *Feed the faeries*.

"I will, I promise—but you be safe!" shouted Luka, ignoring the heads that turned in his direction and the tears that sprang to his eyes. "Just . . . be safe!"

She climbed on board, and a moment later the door clicked shut. Hugo whined.

Luka opened his phone and read the War Effort text, focusing on the words YOUR FAMILY'S FATE.

The train slid under the station's roof of iron and glass, and he waved the palmed coin over his left hand, appearing the silver disk as if by magic—then passed his right hand back across his palm.

The coin vanished.

Luka plunged his empty hand into the fur on Hugo's neck and watched until the train disappeared between domino tower blocks, its windows bright with the hard winter sky.

2

For all these chores and many more
They ask but just one thing
A plate of bread, with milk besides
For that, you'll hear them sing!
But should you take their gifts for grant
An enemy you'll make . . .
Do not mistake their work for love
They give—but they can take!

Traditional song, anonymous

As he left the concourse and crossed the square, Luka snapped his headphones over his ears and found his favorite playlist—music his dad had loved—and tried to imagine what Elena would be seeing soon: cows, trees, rolling quilts of fields and pasture.

He looked about and found, instead of familiar streets, the hot-running engine of War: trucks and canvas and uniformed staff, lights in the sky, bomb-damaged roads, and the ever-urgent hum of helicopters weaving through the dark, glowering sky towers—the mile-high sentinels that bordered Bellum City.

Luka blinked. It was as though, without Elena, the

City had shifted its muscles and was casting a threatening light, its skin newly clad in armor.

Hand clutching Hugo's fur, he crossed between the buses on North Street, his breath held against the rumbling exhaust. The trucks and Wardens were gone, and the ruined houses gaped like carcasses. By nightfall, they would be infested with looters, seeking not iron and scrap but gold, silver, and other sellable goods.

He thought of what Elena had said as he approached Wildwood Park: that the faeries didn't care about the War, they just wanted to be fed. The idea was strangely comforting—a point of constancy amid the chaos—and he allowed himself to lean into it as he and Hugo trudged up the hill toward his house.

"What you smiling at, Rake?"

Hugo barked and pawed the ground. Luka swore under his breath.

"Why do you have to call me that?" he said, removing his headphones and looking around. He had meant to take the path on the other side of the park, far away from Hazel's tumbledown watchtower—but had wandered, thought-blind, right into it.

"Thin as a rake, in't you?" said Hazel, tugging Luka's earlobe.

Luka jumped back, hand clamped to the side of his head. "So are you."

Hazel—lean and dark-skinned, his hair a crown of dark curls—dropped from a crumbling archway and crouched over his firepit. An old coffee can, its design faded and scratched, was simmering in its coals. "We all are, I guess," he said, stirring his broth with a twisted fork. "But I mean to put a dent in my rakeness shortly."

A few onions bobbled on the can's surface. Luka smelled pepper and meat.

"What is that?" he said.

Hazel raised his fork, a crow dangling from its prongs. The bird's flesh was tight and gray, and the beak—starkly black against the white skull—hissed with fatty bubbles. Hugo whined and smacked his chops.

"Good, strong bird," said Hazel, his eyes bright. "*Old*. Wartime's made him tough. Been cooking him nearly six hours. Starting to smell pretty good."

"Urgh," said Luka.

Hazel dropped the crow back into the stew. "Meat is meat is meat is meat is meat," he said, scratching Hugo's chin and making the big dog's leg twitch. "You think what you're eating is chicken? Try rat. Or *cat*. You need to see what's in front of you, Rake. Deal with the real."

"We don't eat cats."

"Everyone does under siege. First the rodents, then

the pets—in the pot. Pet. Pot. Petpot." Hazel, grinning in the half-light of his hideout, nuzzled Hugo's wet nose and laughed. He sniffed his stew, opened one of the pockets on his overalls, then threw in a pinch of what he found into the can.

"That your sister gone?" he said.

Luka gave him a hard look. "How do you know that?"

"I see everything, up on my hill," said Hazel, gesturing around his lost-boy den.

Luka peered through the scrapheap web of nets and ropes to the City sprawled below—a garland of barrage balloons strung on its skyline.

"I told you before to stop spying on us," he said, squeezing his fists. The coin dug into its familiar groove on his palm.

Hazel leaped to his feet and pressed his face into Luka's, grinning as the older boy stumbled back.

"Or what?" he said. He went to another pocket and sprinkled crumbs of instant coffee onto his tongue.

"Where do you get that?" said Luka.

"I have my sources," he said, teeth smudged and brown. "You think *I'm* going to drink *chicory root*?"

"You're a thief."

"Bombs are on the way, and you're standing there worrying about my coffee."

"What do you mean bombs are on—"

"Think you're safe here?" said Hazel, grabbing a

low-hanging net and doing a series of effortless pull-ups. "Nu-uh. The Islands are waaaay safer. Way way way way safer."

"What would you know about it?"

Hazel blinked slowly, then, with a gymnastic spin, dropped to the ground and stirred his stew as though nothing had happened.

"What was that?" said Luka.

"A flicflac," said Hazel casually, "also known as a backward handspring."

"You're a gymnast?"

"I am many things." Hazel lifted the steaming crow, peeled off a chunk of flesh, and chewed it thoughtfully. "You can come in and sit. Plenty of space on the log."

"I'm not going to 'sit' with you. This place is a mess."

"This place is *history*, Rake. It was a watchtower when this was all forest: the Wild Wood—that's why this park is called—"

"Wildwood Park, yeah, I get it. But—"

"In World War II," said Hazel, twisting a section of his hair, "this was an anti-aircraft post—you can still see the bolts in the stone. Now there's a new War, and here I am—master of the tower. I'm keeping a noble tradition alive, bro."

Luka looked around the ruin.

"How can you live here?" he said. "Where do you even wash?"

"Oh, under my arms, behind my ears, between my—"

"I *meant* where do you—"

Hazel laughed. "I know what you meant, Rake."

Luka flushed. "You're not meant to be here, you know," he said. "If they found you, they'd—"

"They're not going to *find* me! You're the only one who ever comes here."

Luka narrowed his eyes and pulled Hugo to his side. "I only came here by accident."

Hazel pointed the crow's beak at Luka, and scowled.

"You think you're so superior, with your roof and your carpets and your . . . online gaming! But your whole damn world is falling apart."

Luka frowned, then crouched to settle Hugo's anxious whine. "We live in the same world, Hazel."

"No, we don't. You live there"—he pointed through the trees, toward the houses—"and I live here. But I have everything I need," he added. "More than you think I've got, too. I see everything, you know. *Ev-ry-thing.*"

"Oh, yeah?" said Luka, taking a deep breath and shifting the weight from his weak leg. "And what do you see now?"

"Storm clouds," said Hazel, without looking up. He took a big bite of crow.

Luka ran home through the downpour, listening to the rain on the shelter's tin roof.

3

First, they'll tear your hair away
Each strand pulled nice and slow
Then they'll take your fingernails
One by one they'll go . . .
Their sharpened sticks will spear your gut
They'll draw your precious blood
They'll tear the tongue from out your mouth
And cast it in the mud.

Traditional song, anonymous

Luka spent the next few hours picking at his homework like a mouse at a loaf, his mind seizing, as it always did, when confronted with numbers and formulae. Instead, he practiced coin sleights—palms, sleeves, and French Drops—eventually abandoning his textbooks in an undignified pile when the door slam announced his mum's return from work.

He took the stairs three at a time and barged into the kitchen.

It had been his granny's house and traces of her clung to it like barnacles: old plastic light switches, an ironing board older than Luka, and behind the TV, wallpaper faded by time and sun. An espresso machine and a four-slot toaster sat on the old worktop, lit by an

LED bulb that glowed through an ancient lampshade. It was as though the modern world had been applied to the place only in scraps and patches, and its creaking bones shone through.

Luka had lived in this house his whole life, right on the border of the Old and New Towns that each made up half of the City. Curling, ancient spires and sleek modern glass sat on either side of his roof, the two sides of Bellum's rugged face.

"How did it go today?" said his mum, kissing him on the forehead.

"Fine," said Luka. "She made the train in time."

She leaned out from the fridge, one eyebrow curling up.

"It was close?"

Luka shrugged.

"She made it," he said again, palming his coin and appearing it from behind her ear.

She laughed and mussed his hair, then, microwave beeping shrilly, handed him a red-hot plate.

Luka lifted a piece of stringy, gray meat and shook his fork.

The meat wobbled.

"What is this?" he said.

"Chicken," said his mum, sipping her chicory coffee. "Aren't you hungry?"

Luka pushed the plate away.

"No," he said. Hugo nudged his elbow.

"Need to eat when you can," said his mum, already typing at the dining table. "There *is* a war on. Think of those poor families stuck in the North."

Luka looked over her shoulder, at the TV news. It was filled with the billowing clouds of air strikes and gridlocked traffic on one side of a highway, people signaling frantically to the news helicopter. Dropping the chunk of meat in Hugo's bowl, he wrapped his plate in cling film and put it beside the leavings of earlier rations in the fridge: curling vegetables, one sausage, a block of shiny orange cheese, a jug of milk, a pot of butter that was mostly vegetable oil, and a mound of tripe—thick as folded linen.

His phone buzzed. He grabbed it, but it was just another War Effort text:

> DIGITAL CURFEW AT SUNSET (5:24PM)

"What if Ellie doesn't text before the curfew?" he said.

"Then we'll hear from her tomorrow," said his mum.

"What if she doesn't have Wi-Fi?"

"They will."

She was trying to sound relaxed, but Luka could hear the tension in her throat. He opened his mouth to push her on it, and the fight shimmered between them. But he poured a glass of milk instead and stuffed a slice of bread into the pocket of his sweats.

"I know she'll be okay," he said, giving his mum a one-armed hug. "I'm just . . . you know. I'm sorry."

"That's all right, *patatino*," she said, gripping his forearm. The TV picture changed to drone footage of a taped-off crime scene flickering with blue light. "Another looting, when the world's already falling apart. Your sister's safer on the Islands."

Luka watched the headlines scroll along the info banner:

MAYOR CALLS FOR CALM——CITY IN PANIC——

LOOTING GANGS STRIKE AGAIN——

"Should I change the channel?" he said. "*Anything's* got to be better than——"

"No, thank you," she said, sliding the remote out of his reach. "No sense hiding from it, is there? And if I miss something that comes up in work tomorrow . . ."

She gave up on the sentence and gestured with her papers.

"Okay," said Luka, seizing on her distraction. "I'm going upstairs."

Hugo leaped to his feet with a snare of claws on linoleum.

"Not too long on your games, then," she said, sipping her now-cold chicory coffee and pulling a face. "The power ration's almost gone."

Luka dropped into his gaming chair as the sun sank into the City, forming a halo around a barrage balloon before plunging behind the cathedral's spire. Steam rose from the great, pot-bellied sky towers, their edges merging with the gloom, red light glowing through the clouds as they scanned the darkening horizon.

Hugo rolled on the rug, released a gentle fart, then fell asleep.

Fifteen minutes passed, unfelt, the voices in Luka's headphones muffled by the noise of his thoughts as he completed mission after mission of *Final Crisis IV*, his thumbs moving on their own. He checked the window, then his phone.

5:19 p.m.

Nearly sunset—and still no message.

He kicked off the game and sat for a moment in silence.

"Told you it was gonna rain."

Hazel's voice buzzed into Luka's head like a drill— he snatched off the headphones in surprise and stood, knocking over his chair.

Tinny laughter rang up from the floor.

"Hazel?" said Luka, leaning down.

"Hello, Rake," said Hazel. His voice sounded scratchy, like an old recording. "How was your 'chicken,' then?"

"It wasn't . . ." Luka hit the buttons of his dead

controller and watched his avatar fall, helplessly, under a storm of blows. "How are you doing this? Have you got"—Luka knew how stupid he sounded, but couldn't stop himself—"*Final Crisis IV*?"

Hazel laughed so hard that Luka had to hold the earpiece at arm's length until he'd stopped.

"Do I look like I play *computer* games?" he said eventually. "I told you—I deal with the *real*, man. You should read more—they can't put a curfew on the mind."

"Then *how* are you—"

"I see everything, right? Well, I hear a lot of things, too. Like how your mum agrees with me that the world's falling apart."

Luka's chest tightened.

"Are you *spying* again—"

"Curfew's up," said Hazel. "See you tomorrow."

There was a *click*—and then silence.

"Tomorrow?" said Luka. He checked his phone.

5:24 p.m.

Curfew had begun. The sun's last glow winked out, and darkness fell.

Night meant something different now. A few years ago, before the War, Luka's street had been warm with orange fluorescence and headlit cars. Now the blacked-out City disappeared behind shuttered windows and dampened bulbs. The dark slithered with primordial power beneath a star-white sky; ruffians moved like eels through the newborn shadows, making knifepoint robberies and black-market trades, scattering seeds of fear wherever they went.

Luka crossed the hallway to Elena's room.

Already it seemed frozen in time—the hairbrush and stuffed animals and bedclothes were no longer just things, they were *her* things, dropped where she'd left them. Her absence stuck like a pebble in Luka's throat and he felt sore with the false calm that filled every room in the house. He and his mum now had to tread around the ghosts of both his father and sister, each consumed by the War. First his dad, shot on the front line wearing a doctor's armband; now Ellie, banished to the supposed safety of the Islands.

Luka opened her window, holding the milk and the bread.

Her previous offering was on the windowsill, but the saucer was empty. Luka's heart beat double for a moment—until he saw the bird droppings.

For a half second he'd thought the faeries *had* been there, *had* taken the food Elena left for them. But of course the gulls had taken it—sometimes they tried to grab sandwiches out your hand. A plate of crumbs wouldn't last long.

Luka pressed the bread onto the saucer and poured the milk over the top, its gentle glug the only sound in the world.

Until the first bomb landed.

The explosion took a moment to reach Luka's ears, but then it knocked him on his back as the bombs flashed like buttercups on the distant cloud-bellies. At first they burst with silent color, thundering into his sister's room and fluttering the posters on the wall as Hugo yelped in terror.

"Luka!" shouted his mum. "Shelter—*now!*"

"I'm coming!" Luka called back, bomb light red on his skin—and on the saucer of milk.

He gritted his teeth.

Food for faeries was a game.

This was real. Bombs. War.

Elena.

Anger moved through him like hot steam that boiled from his guts into his veins.

"No!" he screamed. "NO!"

He threw the saucer at the bombers, watching the bread and milk arc toward the moon—then drop on the oak tree outside her window with a sharp *hiss*.

He slammed the window shut.

Later, in the shelter, sleep came like a slow fog. Luka dreamed he was on the Islands with his sister and his dog, watching bombs fall on the horizon and running his hand over cool grass.

Outside, fire poured on the City, and the faeries' milk dried on the bark.

4

Steam rose, bright with moonlight, from the rabbit's breathless mouth. Jem dropped the animal's slack head and licked blood from his knuckles. Crows glistened in the skeletal trees, clicking their beaks.

Waiting.

The faerie checked his reflection in the waist-high marble of the rabbit's eye, then lifted the paring knife from his goat-horn pack and savored the tinny smell of hot blood in the cold air.

Midnight. Esme said the offering had been spilled. She had already marked the boy's house.

Good, thought Jem. *It has begun.*

He peeled the soft, warm skin and tossed it to the birds. Then, sirens ringing in the distance, he snapped the front legs and stripped the silver sinew, as fine and clear as snakeskins, from the delicate ribs.

Blood dripped black between his fingers, and moonlight glowed through the rabbit's bones.

Jem threw the fat and gristle to the flutter of crows; then, spiders climbing over his boots, he reached into the belly and scooped out the organs before stuffing the dripping mass into his pack.

He cleaned his blade and pushed the hair from his face, leaving a smear of blood on his pale skin.

"Done," he said.

A crow, purple and blue in the morning sun, landed beside him. Jem looked up into its eyes.

The bird stepped back, feet padding anxiously on the frost.

"A lift, please, corvid," said Jem, strapping the bloody horn to his back. He waited for the crow to drop a wing, then hopped between its wings and took its neck in his hands.

"Fly," he whispered.

The crow leaped into the air, carrying the faerie over the human City, weaving through columns of bomb smoke and fire.

5

When, eventually, they returned to their beds, Luka gripped his phone and waited for the network to come back. He saw strange movement in the moonlight as he moved in and out of sleep; quick shapes that vanished under focus, like fish in a sunlit pond.

Time passed and the sun rose and the shadows disappeared.

The buzz of a message roused him, and he sat up groggily. Hugo, lying on his legs, grunted and reluctantly shifted position.

Ellie: ☺

Luka's hand shook as he thumbed open the app.

> Hi Lukie! Got here no prob. Ferry made me a bit sick but didn't throw up!! Feel weird now, kind of weak 😫 It's a bit strange (there's loads of us in a big dorm, I'm in a bottom bunk) but there's animals everywhere which is cool! 🐮🐿
> I hope you and mum are alright don't worry bout me I'll be fine. Did you feed faeries?
> Miss u Exx

Good news you're there ok and there's animals — how many kids are there in the dorm? was freaking out a bit when you didn't text 1st night. Was a bomb raid (you prob saw it?) so me an mum were in shelter until midnight. Off today as teachers on duty so txt later OK? Lx

He waited a moment to see if Elena started typing back. When she did not, he got up and started dressing—same clothes as the day before, different socks.

His skin smelled like the dank, underground concrete of the bomb shelter. Even with the windows tightly closed, the smell of the raid filled the room: acrid bomb-stink mixed with burning carpet and paper.

There would be no school today. Every teacher had another job immediately after a raid—fire warden, search and rescue, recovery, identification—so there were no lessons for the day. The school itself was open all day, even on weekends, but only as an overflow for the hospital.

One morning in homeroom, Luka had taken his seat to find a tuft of cotton wool snagged on his desk like sheep fleece on barbed wire—and a long pair of scissors covered in dry blood. He found out later that a jet had been shot down during the night and the pilot's surgery had been carried out on his desk.

Luka pictured those dark, fresh stains now, and wondered what to do until lunchtime. The thought of playing *Final Crisis IV* was strangely unwelcome. Hazel's mockery of the game had bugged him. He was living a real and dangerous life out in his tower, while Luka played safely indoors.

Maybe he'd go back there, show Hazel he wasn't scared of him. Of *anything*.

See you tomorrow.

Hazel's final words rang in Luka's memory. But *how* had he known that—

The doorbell chimed.

Hugo barked and spun in excited circles. Luka checked his phone again, then hopped down the first flight of stairs to answer the door, stopping on the half landing when he heard an official-sounding voice.

"Well, I suppose if—" his mother said.

The woman cut her off.

"Government orders, ma'am. I'm going to most of the houses on your street. Bad one last night. Lots of people on the move."

"It's just that the room is still . . . She only left yesterday, and—"

"An empty room is an empty room. Sign here, please . . . Thank you."

Luka heard a pen lid snapping into place, followed by the *whirr* of her fingerprint on the Warden's tablet.

"What's his name?" said his mum.

"Fleming. Max Fleming. He's eleven—looks older though."

"When is he coming?"

"He's already here," said the woman. "We've got two coaches at the bottom of the road. He'll be with you in a few minutes."

His mum took a long, deep breath.

"Right," she said.

The door closed.

Luka jumped onto the banister and slid toward her.

"What's happening?" he said. "Who was that?"

His mum looked tired. She never slept in the shelter—just sat up through the darkness, willing the bombers away.

"A Domestic Warden," she said, "on relocation duty. We're getting a resettler. Max."

"What? We can't be—"

"Luka, I don't—"

Luka followed her to the kitchen, cutting her off.

"Where are we going to put him?" he said, pulling her sleeve. "It's not like we've got a huge house, and—"

"He's going to stay in the spare room."

Luka blinked.

"What spare room?"

She gave him a look. "The Islanders have welcomed Ellie into their home, now we're going to do the same for this poor boy."

Luka felt as though his stomach had been slit open. He gripped the doorframe.

"But—" he began.

"I don't want any complaints from you, Luka Maldini—*non sei capace di tenerti un cece in bocca!*"

"I can so keep my mouth shut! But what if Ellie—"

"Elena is staying there until the end of the War, and if I could I'd send you with her."

"I don't—"

"Enough, please. I got an email this morning," said his mum, taking his hand. "I've to go away for a few days—some of the fortifications on the coast need a survey."

Luka's shoulders dropped.

"You're leaving? When some kid's coming to stay?"

She thinned her lips and breathed out quickly through her nose. "I've got no choice, Luka. You know that."

"I know, but—"

"Another Domestic Warden will come and check on you at eight sharp every night, the same as last time."

"Ellie was here the last time," said Luka, knowing it was stupid and unfair but saying it anyway.

"We all have to do difficult things," said his mum, lifting her briefcase. "Your *papà* did difficult things."

Luka felt the specter of his dad standing between them, watching them with patient eyes.

"Mum—"

The doorbell chimed, and this time it seemed to echo through the house.

His mother snapped her briefcase closed and ruffled Hugo's ears.

"This poor boy was bombed out during the night," she said, "and I know I'd be damn grateful to anyone who took you in if our house had gotten hit, so you be welcoming."

The doorbell chimed again.

"On you go," said his mum.

Luka walked past his mum's overnight bag, watching the dark shape in the door's frosted glass.

He gripped the handle.

"Luka . . ." said his mum, appearing behind him.

Luka opened the door.

A dirty face peered up at him, eyeholes rubbed from a cracked mask of mortar and soot. Max, slumped on an enormous duffel bag, smelled of flames and smoke, his clothes slabbed with dust and dirt. Pale skin showed on cheeks cleaned by tears, and the whites of his eyes were pink and raw. His thumb was wedged in the pages of a yellowing book, and he sat completely still.

"Come in!" said Luka's mum, appearing at his shoulder. "God above, you're welcome here, come in!"

Hugo nosed Max's hand, his thin tail moving uncertainly.

Luka's mum nudged his ribs.

"Hello," said Luka, his stomach tensed. "Hi."

Max stomped inside, eyes on the floor. He wore his rage like a diver's suit: heavy and thick and so completely closed off he seemed not to have seen Luka or the house or anything at all.

"Maybe you could take the case up the stairs," said his mum.

Max lifted his head and stared past them.

"It's really heavy," he said, his northern accent thick. "I'll get it."

"It's no trouble," said Luka, pulling the handle.

It didn't budge.

"*I'll* get it," said Max again, lifting the immovable bag with a single grunt.

"Show Max to Elena's room," said Luka's mum. "The Domestic will be round at eight. Eat *properly*, not just tea and toast—use the ration app and order some veg, all right? Max, you make yourself at home."

She kissed Luka quickly on the forehead.

"I'll see you next week," she whispered. "Be good."

Luka listened to her footsteps vanishing down the path. Max pushed past him, anger pouring off him like thick, dark heat.

"Upstairs?" he said, without turning around.

Luka nodded, then squeezed past with Hugo and led the way, self-consciously hiding his weak leg.

Max followed him, and the smell of the War moved into the house.

At Elena's bedroom, Luka's mind flashed to the bomb-lit silhouette of milk and bread he'd flung from the window, and to his surprise and shame, he froze—like a mouse flattened by a passing shadow.

Instinctively, he palmed and reappeared his coin, listening with all his senses to the silence on the other side of the door.

"What are you waiting for?" said Max.

"Nothing," said Luka, opening the door. "Here's the room. Don't—"

The words stopped in his throat.

Before the War started, Luka had been chased from school by an older boy who'd thrown bricks at his bedroom window. But no panes were smashed and there was no broken glass; the bricks had simply bounced off as though they'd struck rubber.

When his dad got home, he'd nodded at the windows.

"Unbreakable," he'd grinned, wolfing his dinner down before going to see the boy's parents. "Triple glazed. Stop a bullet, that stuff."

Luka remembered the sound of bricks ricocheting off the unbreakable glass as he looked at the window in Elena's bedroom, Hugo barking madly at his heels.

It was split by a long, deep crack, and crowned by a smear of blood no bigger than a thumbnail, its tiny shape unmistakable.

A handprint.

6

Luka pulled the curtain across the window as fast as he could and spun to face Max, who loomed, eyes downcast, a soiled crow in the bright doorway.

"Here you are," said Luka, trying to keep the tension from his voice as the words *faerie blood faerie blood faerie blood* hammered like a drum in his head. "My sister's room."

Max dropped the large case at Luka's feet and glowered.

"Right," said Luka. "I'll just—"

But Max was already moving past him. Luka felt the big boy's knots unwinding and bit the inside of his lip as Max, spattered and stained and stinking of fire, sat on his sister's bed. Smoke stung Luka's nostrils as the resettler shed his coat and sweater.

Neither of them made a sound, but Luka felt himself being dismissed by Max's exhaustion and anger.

"This is my sister's room," he said again, raising his voice over the *faerie blood* drumbeat, "so while you're here—"

Max, his face terrible under its mask of soot, his eyes trembling and wet, stood and knocked Luka onto his backside.

"This is *my* room," he growled, chest heaving as Hugo barked around them. "I've been bombed out *three times*—I haven't even washed the last one off me yet. So if you think I'm going to sit and let a little prick like you boss me about, you're dead wrong." He saw Luka glance at the scars on his chest. "Get out then! Go!"

Luka climbed to his feet and stood for a moment, moving his coin from hand to hand as Max turned his back and began to strip, peeling bomb-dark clothes from skin that was brightly pink and smelled of tired sweat.

He shook his head and reached for Max's shoulder.

"Don't you *dare* tell me to—"

Max's arm uncoiled like a viper, driving his fist high into Luka's stomach. Hugo barked and growled, backing himself into a corner of the room.

Luka felt as though a balloon had inflated in his belly. Writhing on the floor and grabbing for Max's ankles, he tried desperately to fill his flat lungs.

"Stay out of *my* room," said Max, pushing Luka and Hugo out and slamming the door. "Don't even *look* at me!" he added through the wood.

Luka rolled onto his knees, his nose touching the carpet, inhaling dust in slowly expanding breaths and blinking back frustrated tears. Max's angry shuffling came to him through the floorboards, an arrhythmic beat against the quiet notes of his house.

He wanted to cry. But the nation's children had been evacuated: to the Islands, the Highlands, the Lakes.

Luka was no longer a child.

He swallowed the tears, went into his room, and wrote a text to his sister.

> New boy moved into your room (bombed out 💣) already. I'll keep an eye on him, so don't worry. Hope OK down there. Text me when you can xx

"Some guard dog you are," he told Hugo, nosing his hand as he pocketed his phone. "Aren't you supposed to defend me?"

"Mornin', Rake."

Luka jumped. Hazel's tinny laughter hissed up from the headphones on the floor. Luka scrambled them onto his ears.

"Hazel?" he said. "How are you doing this? I'm not even logged in to—"

"Oh, you never know who's listening," said Hazel.

Luka remembered Elena mimicking the advert, and felt a stab in his bruised guts.

"Bit of damage to your house," Hazel carried on. "You get bombed out, like me?"

"Damage? In the raid?"

"Your windows, Rake."

"What do you—" Luka began, his eyes refocusing on the window of his own room.

More broken glass—and another tiny, blood-stained handprint.

Faerie blood faerie blood faerie blood faerie blood, Luka thought. Then, staring past the bloody print to the bomb-damaged City, oozing like a burst and broken engine, he saw Hazel's tower in the foreground—the branches around it bent toward Luka's house by the west wind.

"Hazel!" he shouted, pulling the breath back into his flattened lungs. "God, this wasn't the . . . You did this, didn't you? *You* did it!"

"Eh? Did what?"

"Don't lie!" Luka shouted, throwing the headphones to the floor and hurrying downstairs with Hugo at his heels. He ran through the lingering smell of his mum's perfume in the hall and his warm, breakfasty kitchen, into the acrid bomb-wind that whipped across the park.

Hazel popped into view as he approached the tower.

"What you doing up here so early, Rake? No school today, eh, so—"

"You did it, didn't you?" shouted Luka, grabbing at Hazel's ankles.

Hazel darted away, slipped, and landed on his back.

"Hey! Urgh—" he grunted, then flipped onto his feet. "What are you *talking* about—"

"Why are you spying on us?"

"I'm not . . . not . . . spying," said Hazel, leaping back as Luka came at him again, "I just . . . listen in, sometimes. Not meaning anything bad, like, but I get lonely and—"

"So, you admit it?" shouted Luka, pushing him back to the ground. "So, what are you trying to do? Mess with my head?"

"Your head?" said Hazel, eyebrows furrowing. "What the hell are you talking about?"

"Last night, when you were eating that bloody crow, you told me you '*see everything*'! Are you sick? You want to torment me now my sister's gone, is that it?"

"What are you *talking* about?" cried Hazel, leaping onto a pile of stones.

Luka jumped as high as he could, grabbing for Hazel's feet.

"Stop—*spying*—on—us!" he screamed, his belly still bruised and sore from Max's fist. To his horror, tears welled in his eyes. Then, as he blinked them away, he saw a Warden emerge from the hedgerow, a cigarette hanging from his lips, leaves tossing in the wind behind him.

Hazel followed Luka's gaze. His eyes widened.

"Don't," he said. "If they find me here . . . Rake . . . Luka, you can't—"

The Warden, face hidden in his helmet's shadow, took a long pull of his cigarette. Luka saw the man's eyes flash in the red glow, and felt the knot of anger— at Hazel and Max and the War and Elena being taken away—coil tighter in his belly.

Hazel dropped from his branch and took Luka's hand.

"He'll take me away if he finds me!" he whispered. "They'll put me in some home and make me go to school! Don't do this, I'll stop the spying and the watching, I don't mean anything bad by it, but I—"

Luka watched the Warden scan the park.

"He'll be doing a check of the area," he said, looking directly at Hazel. "Looking for anything that shouldn't be here."

Hazel took a panicked breath.

"Listen, Rake," he said, "I know you're mad at me, but don't do this. *Please.*"

The Warden ground the cigarette under his boot and turned to go. Luka raised his phone and took a picture.

And there, captured on his screen, was Hazel: living out in the open, his eyes wide and scared, his hands raised in supplication. Luka saw the briefest flash of his sister's gentle eyes in Hazel's desperate face, and felt her gaze upon him, seeing what he was about to do.

He released the shout for which he'd drawn breath and stepped back, shaking his head.

"I won't—"

Luka's heel struck a tumbled rock and he fell, striking his head and crying out as Hazel wailed and the Warden, eyes flashing in the dark of his visor, came running.

7

A few miles away in a thatched roof in the Old Town that smelled of cedar and cinnamon, a gathering had begun.

Five chairs sat round a cake-stand table, each containing a well-dressed figure no bigger than a can of beans. More shapes—the squires and servants and armored rats of the Elder Guard—lurked beyond the candle's reach, and the air crunched with grinding teeth.

"But it's on *your* territory," said a tiny man, testing a hatpin on his thumb. "What's being done about it?"

"Plenty, *Lord* Doller," growled the woman opposite. Like him, her face was hard—skin stretched fleshlessly over sharp bones. "So you'd best button those flapping lips."

Doller took a slow bite of a pomegranate seed.

"This question is valid, Lady Esme," said the Gray Lady, her face gnarled under a bun of hair. "What of the broken pact?"

Esme adjusted the rosemary in her lapel, then held up the fresh wound on her palm.

"The house is marked by my blood. It is of no importance."

"No importance?" spluttered Rudge, all powdered face and beaky nose, his pine-frond hat shaking with fury. "The boy threw the offering on the *ground!* It hit our oak tree!"

"And one of my houses will enact the cost."

Doller dabbed juice from his chin and leaned forward. "Who?"

"My best," said Esme.

Boots rang on the floor. The new man who approached the table was short, even among fairfolk, and as he walked he bit the end from a shard of slate, jaws squeaking as tooth met rock. The seated figures winced—all except Esme, who kicked off her boots and grinned.

"Jem?" said Doller.

Jem tossed his horn of rabbit meat onto the table, its lid oozing blood.

"You all know me," he said, flecks of slate on his lips. "You know what I can do."

"And what can you do, traitor?" said Rudge, eyes narrowed.

"Plenty," said Jem, taking another screeching bite.

Doller showed his teeth. "You're all talk."

"And *you're* all hot air. Why don't you kiss your own—"

"Insults have no place at council!" snapped the Gray Lady, slicing into the cake stand with her obsidian sword.

The tip juddered beneath Jem's nose.

"Who's being insulting?" he said. "Lord Doller is a flexible man—I honestly think he can do it."

Laughter murmured through the space. People relaxed back into their coats, and the fur smoothed on the Elder Guard. Doller glared at Jem, then took another bite of his pomegranate.

The Gray Lady jerked the sword from the table with a *drroing* and returned it to her lap.

"Jem's bravery is not in question," she said, "but his record shows a . . . sympathy with the human world—"

"I'm right here, you know."

"—it smells like weakness."

Jem scowled. "That girl was barely walking. Almost a babe in arms—where's the glory in that?"

Rudge shook his head. "The lore is the lore is the lore," he muttered. "What have we if we abandon the rules, if we don't take body parts in exchange for insults? The bigguns will ignore and forget! And then where will we be? We will be lost! The lore is food in our bellies—without it we shall starve. We shall die. Without vengeance for this insult, we shall *die!*"

Low voices rumbled in the gloom, and feet shifted on the ground.

Esme bit her lip.

"The responsibility for this lies with my house," she said. "We have already dealt with the girl of the family. *Elena*. Jem will ensure her brother does not escape punishment. I swear it."

The Gray Lady looked at Jem. "If this boy barricades the house against us, his insult will pass unavenged. This cannot happen."

Crushing the last of his slate in his palm, Jem opened his coat to reveal swords, pliers, and blades.

"This boy—Luka—he knew what he was doing."

The Gray Lady nodded.

"We are aided by the human War, which eats their iron. Our only enemy is their hearts. We are more powerful by far, but love makes humans strong— and with love in their hearts they are capable of great things. We must act fast."

Jem caught Esme's eye and nodded.

"So," said the Gray Lady, pointing her sword at Jem, "you take responsibility for the house, the insult, and the boy?"

Jem's lips twisted over teeth that were sharp and black.

"I do," he said.

8

"*No!*" shrieked Hazel, pushing Luka out of the way and throwing a clutter of junk into a duffel bag.

The Warden was running toward them, whistle gripped shrilly in his teeth.

"Why would you do this to me?" said Hazel, scrambling around his nets and returning with armfuls of sleek-looking gadgets, listing them as they landed in the bag. "Scrambler, decoder, subsonic pistol, graphene knife—"

"I didn't—I fell! I swear I wasn't going to!" Luka shouted back.

"Yeah? Well, you've done it now, Rake," said Hazel, staring past Luka to the approaching Warden. "Up yours," he added; then, with a last desperate look at his lair, he spat at Luka's feet and ran.

Luka watched him vanish into the woods, leaping effortlessly into the safety of the shadows.

The Warden burst red-faced into the den.

"You the one that shouted?" he said, soft chins wobbling.

Luka stepped back, keeping Hugo, growling deep in his belly, behind him. The man radiated menace like a boiler's heat.

"No," said Luka. "I mean, yes. I fell and shouted." Luka watched the Warden's knuckles tighten on his baton. "And that's all I know," he mumbled. He slipped his phone into his pocket, hiding the photo of Hazel's panicked face behind the lock screen.

"This your stuff?" said the Warden.

"No!" said Luka, too quickly. "I live with my mum. She's an engineer. For the Civil Defense Corps."

The Warden pushed past Luka and prodded the nets. He smelled of cigarettes and sweat and dirty clothes. Luka's skin itched with his closeness.

"This is just the kind of thing I'm looking out for," the man sneered, prodding the hammock with a nasty leer. "Kids are living wild in the City, maybe out on the moors. Caught plenty of them, but nothing like this."

Hugo barked, then fell silent under the Warden's deep, black eyes. Luka peered into the darkness of the woods.

Stay hidden, Hazel, he thought.

As though he'd heard his plea, the Warden flashed a humorless smile.

"Can I go now?" Luka said.

The Warden lit another cigarette and funneled smoke through his nostrils. "Where do you live?"

"Over there," said Luka, pointing away from his house.

"Beasley Street? What number?"

"One hundred," said Luka.

The man snorted.

"Easy to remember."

"Yeah," said Luka, then "yeah" again. He backed out of the clearing holding Hugo's collar and ran to his house. Hidden there, in the frosty hedge, he saw the cigarette glow in the gloom of Hazel's den, and shivered.

"What have I done, Hugo?" he whispered, as the big dog nosed his hand.

Back in the kitchen he listened to Max moving about upstairs—boots on the carpet, drawers opening and closing—as he tried to tidy up the breakfast things. He felt as aware of the boy upstairs as he would be of a seed in his teeth, and his eyes kept lifting to the ceiling.

But when he forced them down they drifted to the park, its canopy blowing green and wild in the wind. More Wardens were descending on Hazel's watchtower, and a black van rumbled across the grass.

Luka ran upstairs and slipped through his bedroom door as silently as possible, hoping that Max would stay in Ellie's room—in *his* room.

He could see a host of Wardens in the park now, running UV torches over Hazel's nets and pulling down his ropes. Luka swallowed hard, then knelt to examine the broken, bloodied window.

The handprint was still there, a tiny smear of bright crimson above the latch. Every finger was absolutely perfect: every fold of skin, every rippling print. There was even the mark of a ragged fingernail and a callous on the thumb.

It looked fleshy. Alive.

Real.

No matter how clever Hazel was, no matter how much he might want to mess with Luka, there was no way he could possibly have made such a thing.

Luka felt the speeding of his heart, as though the pace of his own blood had quickened through his veins. A faerie—an actual, living faerie—had stood on the other side of this bulletproof glass and punched it so hard it had split.

"I don't . . . what the . . ." he said, trying to calm the hot lead in his belly as he walked into his mum's room.

It felt normal. Calm and warm, all scented candles and snow globes on the windowsill. Luka looked at the snow globes, thinking about how he'd shake them as a child—seeing now the window above reflected on their bright domes, smeared, as he'd known it would be, with a tiny, bloody handprint.

This one looked more like a claw, he thought, leaning as close to the window as he dared, and there was a deep crack in the middle of the crimson palm, as though a hammer had struck the pane.

Or a fist, he thought, heart beating into his throat.

All at once, the house was surrounded.

A tiny sliver of glass, thin as a fingernail, lay in

the middle of the floor. Luka palmed it quickly, then crossed back to his own room, listening to Max pace and mutter behind Ellie's door.

Luka shifted the broken glass between his fingers and felt its edge, sharp as a wasp sting. Blood sprang between his knuckles. He opened his hand and watched it run across his palm.

No magic, he thought. *No tricks. They're as real as the War—as real as the bombs and everything else.*

He looked outside. Wardens swarming over the park.

"What I am going to do?" he said.

Hugo, sprawled on the bed, yawned and turned over.

Wiping his hand on his jeans, Luka wrote another text to his sister:

> Hey Ellie, hope farm is OK! Just wondering, what happens if you don't remember to feed the faeries? Like, just wondering, in case I forget! Lx

He waited for it to deliver, but instead watched it hang in the space between them—unread and unanswered—and thought about Elena's face as she climbed onto the train, how pleased she'd been when she secured his promise.

"What I am going to *do*?" he said again, leaning

toward the window. "What the hell am I going to—"

A fist smashed into the glass.

Luka fell onto his weak leg and cried out. Hugo barked—then wagged his tail and darted forward.

"Enjoying yourself, Rake, watching them tear my tree to bits?" said Hazel, pulling open the window and climbing into the room.

9

"Hazel?" shouted Luka. "How did you—"

"Not hard to give that big bugger the slip," said Hazel, coffee grains between his teeth. "You can hear those smoker's lungs wheezing a mile away."

"How long have you been out there?"

"Long enough," he said, throwing his bag onto Luka's gaming chair.

Luka's stomach twisted under Hazel's stare. He pressed a handkerchief to his bleeding palm.

"Hazel, I—"

"Save it, Rake—I know what you were doing—and I know why, too."

"What do you mean?"

"You hate me."

"No, I don't! And I fell—I didn't mean to—"

"It's fine. I'm used to it."

Luka's blood soaked through the white fabric. "I don't, Hazel. I don't. I just—"

Hazel put his finger on Luka's lips.

"Wha uh you ooing?" Luka managed, wriggling free and wiping his mouth.

Hazel crab-walked over to the window and withdrew a telescope from his bag like a sword from a scabbard.

"I want to know what they're talking about," he said.

"Who?"

"Them," said Hazel, pointing at the swarm of City Wardens. The sun rose over the City, coating the room in its warm, orange glow. Hazel's face fell into shadow behind his curtain of hair, and Luka watched his slender fingers twist the telescope's dials and buttons.

"I don't see how—"

"How's the new boy?" said Hazel.

"Max? How do you know about—hang on, more spying?"

Hazel shrugged. "I see *everything*," he said, lifting the telescope and peering at the park. "I know he kicked your butt, too. Your fault—don't deny it. Seems like being mean to bombed-out kids is kind of your thing, huh?"

Luka opened his mouth, closed it, and sniffed. Hazel's green, earthy scent was filling the room, as though a plant had sprouted from the carpet and settled into the air.

"My sister's gone," he said eventually.

"Boo-hoo," muttered Hazel. "We've all got problems, Rake."

For a few moments, there was no sound but the clicking of tiny dials as Hazel focused on the Wardens—then Luka heard small voices coming from the telescope.

Nearly done here, said a woman's voice.

"Wait, how are you doing that?" said Luka.

"It's a sonic visualizer," Hazel whispered, turning another dial.

The voice grew louder.

The kid had some serious kit. You seen this?

What? said a man.

"That's the Warden you set on me," said Hazel.

"I didn't mean to, Hazel. I swear, I wasn't going to—"

This military scanner. How's he got his hands on something like this?

A dark-skinned man in a long, gray coat appeared behind the Wardens, his eyes hidden behind disks of frosted glass.

"Ah," said Hazel.

"*Hazel!*" Luka whispered, his pulse quickening. "That's a Trenchcoat!"

I want this boy found, the Trenchcoat said, running a hand over his neat moustache.

Absolutely, sir, said the man. *It appears the boy has been living here for—*

This is about more than the boy, snapped the Trenchcoat. *See that this entire collection is labeled within the hour.*

Hazel let the aperture fall to the floor.

"A *Trenchcoat?* What have you *done?*"

"Lots of things. Stuff stuff stuff stuff stuff. You're on a need-to-know basis, right?"

"But I've never even *seen* a Trenchcoat," Luka said, still staring at the park. "Nobody I know has ever seen one! And they're looking for you!"

"You let me worry about that, Rake," said Hazel. "Your window's broken," he added, pointing to the handprint.

"But—" Luka began. Hazel silenced him with a raised hand, sprinkled more coffee on his tongue, and looked out the window. The Wardens were loading his possessions into a shuddering truck.

"Listen, Hazel, about your tower—" Luka began, moving in front of the faeries' bloodstain.

"Oh, don't worry," said Hazel, leaping to his feet.

"What? Why?"

"You're going to make up for that."

"I am?"

"Oh, yeah. In a big way."

Luka swallowed. "How?"

Hazel stretched like a cat—an expansive curl started in his feet, moved through his spine, and finished in his arms—then put his hands behind his head. He made a show of looking around and grinned.

"What a lovely room," he said. "Where shall I put my stuff?"

"I'm sorry?" said Luka.

"I know you are," said Hazel, patting his shoulder.

"You can't move in *here*!" shouted Luka.

Hazel stood, vaulted onto Luka's chest of drawers, and rapped his knuckles against a poster.

"I already have, Rake. Is this a supporting wall?"

"What? I don't know! Why would you need to—"

"Otherwise my hammock could bring the whole roof down. And we don't want that." He thought for a moment. "I might bump my head."

A stethoscope appeared from one of his boilersuit pockets and he began moving the bell along the wall, knocking every few inches and stepping onto the desk, tipping over a pot of pencils and a half-empty mug of milk.

"Hey!" shouted Luka, snatching his phone away from the advancing spill and wiping it on his top as Hugo lapped at the dripping milk.

Hazel's eyes flashed.

"Nice handset."

"Don't—!" said Luka, but Hazel's hands were too quick, and he snatched Luka's phone before he could step out of reach.

"This *is* nice," he said. "You must have got this before the graphene ration kicked in."

"Give that back *right* now—if my sister texts me then I—"

"Calm down," said Hazel, dropping the phone into one of his pockets.

Luka grabbed Hazel by the collar.

"Give it back!"

Hazel pushed him away and went back to tapping the wall.

"Don't worry," he said, "I'll let you know if it buzzes."

"Don't bother," said Luka. He clapped his hands together then spread his palms to reveal his phone.

Hazel exploded in delight. "Rake—you're a *pickpocket*? Who knew! Do it again!"

Luka stepped back and vanished his phone.

"No," he said, as Hugo nudged his pocket with his nose. "I don't want you turning it into a spy satellite or something. If my sister—"

"Go on," said Hazel. "Do something else."

Luka reached behind Hazel's ear and withdrew a silver flash drive.

"Easy," he said, trying to hide his delight at Hazel's reaction. "You've got so many pockets in that damn thing."

Hazel grabbed his wrist.

"You can't have that—that's worth its weight in diamonds. Truce?" He grinned, squeezing until Luka opened his hand. "Roommates shouldn't take each other's stuff, after all."

Luka sighed. "We're not roommates, Hazel. I'm sorry about your watchtower, I really am—but you *can't* stay here."

"Oh, but I have to—you think I can just find *another*

tree, now that they're all over my stuff? You know how long it took to set up all those nets? No, you've made the decision for me, Rake—I live here now." Hazel lowered his face to the desk and took a slurp of the spilled milk.

"That's about two days old," said Luka.

"Good," Hazel replied, wiping his chin. "Nice and tangy."

Hugo trotted after Hazel, licking the carpet at his feet with long, rasping strokes.

Luka pressed his hands into his eyes until spots danced in his vision. "Hazel, you can't stay in my *house*."

"Why not?"

"Because . . ." *Because I broke my promise to my sister; because the faeries have put a blood curse on my house; because I have no idea what to do.* "Because you're being hunted by Trenchcoats—secret bloody Government agents! And besides, my mum won't—"

"Your mum's not here, though, is she? And when she comes back, you can explain it's because you grassed me up to the Wardens—"

"I can't tell her that!"

Hazel chuckled. "I know, Rake. Anyway," he added, jerking a thumb over his shoulder, "she let *him* move in, didn't she?"

"Who?" said Luka.

"Me," said Max, standing pink and clean and with wet auburn hair in the doorway.

He looked even bigger, as though he'd emerged from a shell of soot and dirt, his arms swelling against his T-shirt as he rubbed Hugo's flapping ears.

"What do you want?" said Luka.

Hazel carried on tapping the wall, tongue moving over his coffee teeth as he grinned. "Brick! This is a perfect hammock spot—I'll be able to see my old den when I wake up!"

Max glowered at him. "Who's the mad kid?"

"Fine line between genius and madness," said Hazel, holding out his hand. "It's an honor to meet the man responsible for the kicking of Rake's narrow butt."

Max frowned.

"We are a society without manners," sighed Hazel, hitting the floor in a backward roll and returning to his telescope. "You're from the North, then?"

"What about it?"

"Who pinched your scone?" said Hazel, clicking a dial on his telescope. "Got to love that accent— everything sounds angry."

Max squared his shoulders. "Yeah, I'm from the North. Came over the border last week and I've been bombed out twice already. So, I'm not really in the mood for dweeby 'tough guys' or mad cavemen in hammocks."

"*Technically* I haven't hung my hammock yet—"

"Who are you calling a dweeb?" said Luka. "Is this because of my leg?"

Max's cheeks colored. "*No*—this is because you made me feel like I was invading your damn house. I don't care about your stupid leg!"

"It's not my fault, you know! A load of medicines got stuck in a blockade when I was little. I had an infection . . . I nearly died! It works fine, it's just not as strong as my other leg. And I bet—"

"All right, Rake—nobody's saying anything about your leg."

"He is!" Luka shouted, cursing inwardly as he felt tears spring to his eyes. "He called me a dweeb!"

"I never meant because of—"

"Let's all calm down!" Hazel shouted, hopping onto the desk as Hugo barked. "Listen, Rake, *listen!* All right, all right . . . Now, why don't you make me a sandwich?"

"You don't live here!" shouted Luka. "And neither does he! This is *my* house, and my sister's house and my mum's! Just get out, both of you!"

Max lunged at Luka, who stumbled on his bad leg and dodged behind his desk.

"I don't want to be here!" he shouted. "I *have* to live here! Didn't you hear me? I've been bombed out *twice!*"

"Be cool, Muscles!" said Hazel, rolling away from

Max's grabbing hands. "The Rake doesn't like other humans close to him."

"Says the boy who lives alone in a ruined tower."

"*Lived*," snapped Hazel, his face darkening. "You got me evicted, remember?"

"You live in a tower?" said Max.

"I live *here*. We're house buddies now—you, me, and Rake. Rake the Turncoat. Rake the Betrayer. Rake the Dishonorable."

Luka felt blood rush to his face, followed by heat behind his eyes. "I didn't mean to . . . I'm going out," he said, forcing calm into his voice as he pressed his coin against his tendons. "Make sure you're gone when I get back. All right? Both of you. Gone."

He whistled for Hugo and spun on his heels, flying down the stairs and out into the morning's bright chill.

10

The faeries washed their faces in the cold dew, watching the three boys argue behind the broken glass and running their fingertips over the offering's spilled milk.

"Their hearts are empty," said Jem. "This is going to be easy."

"You're sure you can do this?" Esme said, hands gripping the trunk as she climbed into the branches.

"You know I can," said Jem.

He slid a polished blade into his boot, tightened the strap—and closed his eyes.

Human lives washed over him in waves of busy sound: televisions, cars, the dull tap of fingertips on touch screens, and the shrill, invisible whine of electric bulbs glowing in their sockets. The Old Town, with its traditions and its hidden places, loomed at his back, comforting and familiar; the New Town on the other side of the house felt cold and empty by comparison.

He sniffed. Humanness was in the smells, too: odors of sweat and soap and growing hair and—everywhere, like a permanent, damp fog—the vegetable stink of boiling food.

War food, Jem thought. The City had smelled different before the bombs. Richer—full of spice and luxury.

Esme touched his shoulder and Jem closed his senses as he'd been taught. The world grew quiet. He opened his eyes. It was like shutting a door, leaving all the music on the other side.

"You're ready for this," said Esme. Her eyes were small and bright in the shadows.

"Then why do I hear a question?"

Esme looked away. "Because you thought that before. *I* thought that before."

"This is different. This boy has insulted us. Last time—"

"Was something you had to do."

"But that little girl—"

"It was not for you to question. You had your instructions. And you failed."

Jem pulled his hat over his eyes. "It will not happen again."

"This is your last chance," said Esme, squeezing his shoulder. "In a week the sister will be ours, but first the boy has to suffer. He cast our offering to the ground, inviting us to eat with the animals. Rudge is right—if the lore goes unavenged, we are done for."

"I know, ma'am."

"The house has been marked by my own blood. Should your compassion for the humans intervene in the execution of your duty again, then I will not be able to protect you."

"I have no compassion," said Jem. "I swear it. My heart is cold."

A bird fluttered into the nest, a bright worm in its beak. The faeries breathed in its scent.

"Nobody breaks the oath twice," said Esme softly.

Jem's knuckles tightened. "I am the Guardian."

"What is your duty, Guardian?"

"To make sure no others claim our quarry."

"What else?"

"To make sure the boy has no protection—no iron to ward off his Reckoning."

"And lastly?"

"To take our revenge."

"Make it so," said Esme, her outline blurring as she passed through the old tree's shadow and into the faerie world. "Make them know us. Make them *bleed*."

"Yes, ma'am." Jem turned to look at his mistress— but found only earth and leaves.

He was alone.

"I will," he said, crouching in the soil, hands deep in the cold dirt.

He could smell the spilled offering; its ghost clung to the bark like slug trail.

An insult. One that could not be endured.

The City's iron harvest had purified the air. He felt light and strong. Gone were the days of horse- shoes on doorways, of nails in honest boots. Humans, he thought, had long since forgotten the old ways.

It made them vulnerable.

Well, the fairfolk would have their price. And there was nothing these boys, these *children*, could do about it.

Jem took a strip of dried rabbit from his pouch, chewing as he filled his pipe. Presently his eyes glowed in the fire of the bowl and he put a stone to his sword, sharpening its blade with slow, methodical strokes, listening to the humans . . . and drawing his plans against them.

11

Luka was three streets away before he thought about where he was going. The blood was too hot in his ears, his breath sharp in his lungs as he ran, blind in his anger.

Rake the Turncoat. Rake the Betrayer. Rake the Dishonorable.

It was his phone ringing that pulled him back from wherever his mind had gone. Hugo nosed his hands as he swiped to answer, his sister's face popping onto his screen.

"Ellie! Oh my God, are you all right?"

Elena laughed softly. "Yes! Well, I felt a bit sick when I woke up, but—"

"Sick how? You look pale." She looked shrunken, he thought, as though she'd gotten smaller overnight. A sick feeling settled into his stomach.

"I don't know . . . It's probably just nerves. Are *you* okay?"

Luka took a deep breath and forced a smile. "Yeah, I am. Yeah. Just we hadn't heard from you, so, you know."

"I know. But I'm here because there's nothing

dangerous on the Islands. Although . . ." She pulled her hair into a bun and began tying it in place.

"What?"

"I saw a mean-looking sheep this morning."

Luka laughed despite himself. "How can a sheep look mean, exactly?"

"Leather jacket. Angry eyes."

"Tattoos?"

"It did!" said Elena, clapping her hands. "It had a number tattooed on its ear!"

"I don't think that counts," said Luka, sitting on a broken wall as Hugo nudged the phone. "But don't do that again—I thought . . . I don't know . . . something bad had happened. How many kids are there?"

"I don't know . . . thirty?"

"What? I thought you were going to a house? Like, someone's home?"

"It's more like a dorm or something. And the guy running everything is so mean—he's really big, so everyone calls him Little John," said Elena, twirling her fringe. "I have to help on the farm in the mornings though. It's so hard—I've only done one shift and my hands feel like they're broken. And it smells *so* bad. And the Wi-Fi is basically nonexistent. Let me see Hugo."

Luka angled the phone so that Hugo could nose the screen, tail wagging as Elena sang his name.

"There's no signal in the dorm," she said, still blowing kisses to the dog, "so I can't watch anything. Literally no apps work. That's why I couldn't text last night."

"So how are you calling now?"

"I sneaked out of chores and came up to the data mast, on top of the big hill."

"Is it really hilly there?" said Luka. He kicked a stone into a bomb crater and rubbed the pins and needles from his weak leg.

"No, there's just the one, but it's really big. I can see the lights on the sky-towers from here."

Luka glanced up at the nearest sky-tower, its lights blinking with brisk purpose, antennae scanning the skies for stealth bombers and missiles. Behind it, barrage balloons bobbed on invisible currents, their tethers creaking.

"Lukie . . . why did you sound so freaked out when I called?"

"Did I?"

"Yeah. You were out of breath. How come?"

Luka opened his mouth and felt the truth's strange weight on his tongue. "We had a raid last night," he said. "I'm just a bit . . . jumpy."

"Yeah, we heard them at supper. I ran outside and saw the explosions in the clouds. I couldn't sleep until I'd heard it was the docklands that got hit."

"That's where the boy in your room came from."

"Oh, right. What's he like?"

Luka thought of how Max had looked standing over him. "Angry," he said. "He's from up North. This is the second time he's been bombed out."

"God. He must be really suffering."

"Yeah," said Luka, swallowing uncomfortably.

"And it's just you and him in the house?"

"Yes," said Luka, and even to his own ears he sounded false, like he'd swallowed a secret the size of a boulder and got it stuck in his throat.

"Lukie, why were you asking about the faeries? You did feed them last night, didn't you?"

"I took the stuff from the kitchen when Mum was working," he said, trying out the lie but finding it brick-like and bitter on his tongue. "Then the bombs came, and I—"

Elena's face exploded into the screen as she grabbed her phone.

"You *forgot*? How could—"

"No!" said Luka, his face coloring. "The bombs came, and I was thinking about you being taken away, and there were *real* bombs, and . . . it all seemed so unfair! So I threw it all away. Into the garden."

Elena's eyes widened. "You spilled the faerie offering? On purpose?"

Luka remembered again the slash of milk against

the sky. "Yeah," he said. "But it'll be all right, won't it? I can just do it next week, can't I?"

Elena covered her face with one hand, and her shoulders began to shake.

"Ellie, oh, God, I—"

"You *promised*! I made you promise and you did!"

"I know! I feel terrible, and now—"

"Now what? Now they've marked the house?"

Luka's heart stopped beating, just for a second—he felt its dead, heavy mass sitting in his chest, pressing down on his motionless lungs.

"What do you mean?" he said.

Elena wiped her nose and blinked tears down her cheeks. "By now they'll have marked the house with blood. They love blood. Is it on the doors?"

"The windows," said Luka, head spinning. "They've broken the windows."

Elena nodded. "You've never believed me. Even when I—"

"I didn't—"

"Listen! This is bad, like, really bad. This world, our world, is like a skin over everything else. All the weird, scary things you read about in stories—they're all real. The faeries are real."

"I know that now. Just before, it seemed—"

She shook her head. "I told you! And that should have been enough."

"So, what happens now?" said Luka after a moment. "I mean, Mum will freak about the broken windows but—"

"I'm going to send you some screenshots from my encyclopedia," Ellie interrupted.

"From what?"

"My book: *The Encyclopedia of the Eldritch.* Hang on."

The screen blurred. Hugo nosed Luka's hand, and a whistle of wind moved through the ruined houses.

"There you go."

Luka opened their chat and thumbed open the first image.

> The faeries (see also: fairfolk) are many things: dignified, taciturn, immersed in tradition and ritual, yes, and also belligerent, savage, and vengeful.
>
> The one thing they are not, have never been, is cute. Traditional images of rosy cheeks and gossamer wings are gross misrepresentations. In reality they are as sinewy and hard as boiled cloth—and cannot fly without animal assistance.
>
> Fairfolk possess a hard-headed single-mindedness that borders on mania. If they want something, then nothing will stop them—not pain or suffering or threats to life—until they have it in their sharp grip.
>
> Blood is hugely important in a faerie's world. They paint their faces with it, use it to make ritualistic symbols in their homes (known as nests, but more akin to a thatch cottage), and sometimes, in battle or victory, even drink it. Blood, and its power, is the very core of their being.

"That explains the handprints," he said. "There's one on every window in the house. In blood."

He heard a strangled sound on her end. "There's something about that in this one."

Another notification popped up.

"Oh, God, Ellie—I get it, they—"

"Read it."

> The one thing the fairfolk cannot stand, simply cannot bear, is a slight. Insults (the closing of windows previously opened to them, the poisoning of offerings, or worst of all, the deliberate spilling of an offering) will be met with the fiercest fury, for the insult is a stain that cannot be tolerated.
>
> Punishments are severe: sharpened sticks pushed into major organs, eyeballs popped from sockets, tongues torn from screaming mouths. First, the offender, the breaker of the pact; then the rest of the household, one by one. Those humans unfortunate or foolish enough to slight the fairfolk will find their bedchambers marked by smears of blood and broken glass, and meet their fate at midnight, following the passage of three moons—three days' time.
>
> Faeries are ruled in chief by two things: a powerful set of ethics and their interest in human agony. Their weakness, if they have one, lies in their admiration of fidelity and sacrifice. Perform an act of loyalty toward a faerie and you will find it repaid tenfold.

"Three days?" said Luka, feeling a creeping panic closing him in. "I've only got *three* days?"

"But they can't come for you before then. That's the law of their lore. All their strength comes from our offerings—anywhere you go you'll find an old story about fairfolk. People tip their caps walking past a stream, add stones to cairns, or set an extra place at the table. And every time a human does one of those things, the faeries there get a little bit stronger. They're bound to us. They *need* us to believe in them."

"What can I do? Ellie, it says they're going to stab my organs with—"

"There's one thing that might work. They're stronger and faster than you, and they're going to come for you. The only thing you can do is try to protect the house."

Images of armed fortresses flashed through his mind—of medieval castles with ramparts and moats. "Protect it? How?"

"Iron. They *hate* iron."

"The metal?" said Luka.

"Yes. It's their kryptonite."

"They have superpowers?"

"No, but the iron is, like, old magic—it makes them weak. Do you remember the horseshoe above Mrs. Bukowski's door?"

"Yes. The Wardens took it for the War Effort."

"That was to keep the fairfolk away. It's like . . . vampires not being able to cross running water."

"I only need a horseshoe?" said Luka. "That's easy! I'm sure we can—"

"But it's *not* easy. You've messed up, Lukie." Elena wiped her eyes with the back of her hand. "Didn't you see what I sent you? 'Worst of all, the deliberate spilling of an offering'—you did that! You *deliberately* spilled the offering! You'll need to put iron around every door and every window. You need to make the house a fortress of iron—or they're going to kill you."

"But . . . the Wardens," said Luka, eyes flashing over the rows of shattered buildings. "They're taking all the iron away! We've handed in most of our pots and pans, and every house that gets bombed has its metal stripped out! They're even cutting down the railings in the park!"

Elena shook her head. "They're taking away the only thing you need, when you need it more than anyone in the world. But this isn't anything to do with the Wardens or the War—this is ancient magic. The faeires were here before the City ever existed, and they'll still be here when it's nothing but dust."

"Ellie . . . why didn't you tell me?"

"I did! I told you so many times—"

"I mean about the punishments, the blood . . . all this. Why didn't you tell me?"

Ellie turned away from the screen for a moment, then looked back—right into his eyes. "Would you have believed me?" she said.

Luka bit the inside of his lip. "No."

"Right. I asked you to do it. That should have been enough." She looked over her shoulder. "I need to go.

Get as much iron as you can to put on the house. Find as much as you can and call me later."

"I will," said Luka, imagining the feeling of a sharpened stick in his side. "I'll fix this," he added, voice breaking. "I promise."

She gave him a look that pierced his heart, then said a taut, hard goodbye that made her feel farther away than ever.

Luka stared around the empty street. Bombed-out houses yawned slackly, soft and dirty from the night's rain. Their roofs looked like torn straw hats, drooping in tangled thatches. What had once seemed so permanent, so *solid*, had been crushed like paper.

But none of that mattered to the faeries. They came and went, through war and winter and disaster, looking for their offerings.

Luka sat staring at his lock screen: a picture of him and Ellie right at the beginning of the War, before she went away, before he'd let her down, before any of this had happened.

12

Luka leaned on Hugo's collar and knuckled his thigh muscle, trying to get his weak leg moving as he took in the shattered remains of the houses around him. The gardens were still squared off into vegetable patches, but the veg was long gone, likely taken by neighbors before the Wardens arrived.

"Iron," he said. "All right. It's not looting if they've been empty for months, is it?"

Hugo barked.

Luka palmed his coin, then tossed it in the air. "Heads, we do it," he said, watching the coin slap onto his palm and releasing a deep breath. "Let's try not to get caught, then."

A boy in the class below him had lived on this street. He'd had stick-out ears that lit up from behind on sunny days. Now he was long gone, his home destroyed in the night when the sky towers missed a single bomber.

Luka climbed into the nearest house, its front wall reduced to a couple of window frames and a gaping basement.

A tideline of damp marked the places the rain had touched, and the whole place smelled musty and dirty.

The carpet was soaked and the kitchen drawers hung open, soft as panting tongues.

Elena's voice rang in his ears, and he thought of the people who'd lived in these rooms, who'd had birthdays and dinners and watched TV together.

He wondered if they'd thought about all that as they died. If their lives had flashed in front of them, the way it was supposed to.

What will I see, he thought, *if the faeries get me?*

Rake the Dishonorable, said Hazel's voice, booming through his mind.

Luka shook his head. A strange, hollow-sounding wind moved through the empty rooms. He peered into the empty drawers and empty cupboards, then climbed the stairs.

Bits of plastic littered the upstairs landing—tubs and toys and remote controls—and broken wood splayed from split walls. Hugo whined and pawed the footprints in the dirt. Looters, Luka realized: the dirt came with the bombs, and the looters followed. The carpet had been stripped in chunks, exposing spongy underlay and the ribs of the remaining floorboards.

The front bedroom had no floor left at all. The little room had some collapsed and soggy furniture, with bedclothes still on the mattresses, clothes visible in the wardrobes, balled-up socks and pants stuffed into drawers. The slots of the bed frame's bolt- and screwholes were empty, like bullet wounds in their sides.

There was a book on the bed. A page had been folded down. Luka puffed out his cheeks and felt his skin shrink on his bones.

Ellie had told him it would be like this. There was nothing metal in sight, not a pot, pan, or strip of wire. Everything—down to the last screw and nail—was gone.

"What am I going to do, Hugo?" he said, gripping the dog's collar.

The bedroom mirror was cracked. Luka took in his split reflection—two versions of himself, neither complete: each with one eye, one ear, one half of a mouth.

A growl started in Hugo's chest.

Luka crouched and scurried behind a chest of drawers, his weak leg folded painfully beneath him, Hugo's collar in his fist.

"What is it?" he whispered, eyes on the carpet.

Then he heard them: footsteps on the stairs.

A Warden, he thought.

Looting was a crime.

More footsteps. Two people. Three. Four. *Four Wardens?*

The bedroom door swung open.

Hugo began to tremble as his growl rose again, lips curling from his teeth.

"Shh!" Luka whispered.

"Yeah, *shhhhhh*," sneered a high voice. A bag slammed over Luka's head, pulling him to the ground as Hugo yelped. "There's a good boy."

13

Elena slipped into the dormitory and strapped on her apron.

She could hear the others on the farm—all girls, all evacuees—laboring in the abattoir next door, scrubbing and hoisting and shifting the vast crates of packed meat over the concrete floor.

"And just where have you been?" said a deep voice behind her.

Ellie took a breath to steady her voice. Her night had been sleepless and sore, and now it felt like the iron fixtures in the walls and ceiling were *pulling* at her, like a magnet dragging on the tissues beneath her skin.

"I felt faint," she said. "So, I went outside. For a breath of air."

"You've been gone awhile. You think you're special?"

"No."

"You think you're *better* than the others? That they should do *your* work?"

"No!"

Little John moved in front of her. Ellie stared at the single tooth in the foreman's mouth—a flat incisor the color of an unwashed teapot, surrounded by vivid pink gums.

"You best get back in there then, don'cha think?" he said.

Head down, shrinking herself so that there could be no further reason for him to shout or keep her there a second longer, Elena tiptoed past the seething giant and ran into the shed. She stepped quickly over the streams of urine and blood and animal dirt, taking up her broom and joining the rest of the girls as the other men moved around them, bolt guns loose on their hips, and the air filled with the terrified clamor of penned beasts.

14

The bag smelled of vegetables and dirty hair. Luka's face was full of his own breath.

He'd been thrown into a metal box, which he'd assumed was a Warden's van—until he heard the whirr of bike wheels. There were whistles and clicks. Then a long call, like a bird of prey, and they started moving.

Nobody spoke, they just made little noises and swung left or right, throwing him blindly against the walls of the box. He tried to track where he was going.

Right. Left. Left. Left. Right. Left. Left. Left.

We're going in circles, he thought, crashing forward as they slammed to a halt.

Rough hands hauled him to his feet. His weak leg had gone to sleep and he dropped his knees.

"Here he is," hissed a high voice. "Found him in the houses. Looting."

It was a boy, Luka realized, not a Warden or an adult. Even through the bag he could tell the boy was his age.

But, even as the relief washed over him, Luka felt a cold tremor of fear.

Where *were* the adults?

"On your feet, scum." The boy giggled.

He sounded raw, untamed—his voice a frantic bird, giddy and shrill without its cage.

"Where's my dog?" said Luka.

"We ate him," said another boy, younger than the first.

"You didn't!" shouted Luka. He could sense bodies around him as he was marched over uneven ground, sweaty fingers gripping under his arms. "Hugo!"

A clutch of hands threw him forward.

"Get that thing off him," said a new voice. Still a boy, but he sounded older.

The bag was pulled away, scraping Luka's nose and crushing his lips. Light flooded his eyes, and he shielded them with his hands.

"Yes," said the older boy. "Hide your face, child. You may not yet look upon me."

Luka spat the sharpness from his mouth. He recognized the blue carpet beneath him and the smashed wooden benches on either side.

The old church. This is where my aunt got married— where my school awards were handed out. This is their gang hut? No wonder people think it's haunted.

"What do you want?" he said.

"We? *You* were in *our* territory. A spy? A thief? Or some unholy—"

"That's not *your* territory! Those are people's homes!"

The boy sniffed. "Such anger. You may look up now, child."

Luka squinted into the light. A thick-necked boy perched atop the old, fire-ravaged pulpit—sitting on a junk-pile throne of springs and tin drums and balding tires.

Luka gazed around. The whole church, lit by shafts of thin light from its rooftop windows, was a sprawl of garbage—every pew, aisle, and windowsill, even the marble altar, groaned under a tower of rusting iron.

The enormous stained-glass window cast the boy in shadow, and Luka saw two little horns rising from his head.

"Pity," said the boy. "I hoped for a stronger jaw-line."

"What's wrong with my jaw?"

"It'll be broken soon," the boy snorted, "if you don't bite your tongue."

Chuckles rumbled through the shadows. Luka guessed there were fifteen more boys in the church—maybe even twenty.

Too many to run from.

How could this be ten blocks from my house? he thought, massaging his weak leg. *The church looks completely abandoned.*

"What's your name, child?" said the boy.

Luka thought about lying, but his hesitation drew another snort. "Luka."

"Thieves do not fare well here, Luka." The boy rose and descended the pulpit steps, his boots crunching over twisted fenders and rusting tools. "And we *hate* spies. We do not blind, we are not animals. But we will break and bruise enough to . . . discourage . . . offenders."

Luka's eyes darted around, looking for Hugo—looking for an escape.

"Which are you, Luka?" said the boy, lifting Luka's chin with his boot. "Spy? Or thief?"

Luka palmed his coin and took a deep breath. "What's the third option?"

The boy laughed, and the others joined with a gang's shrill, braying laugh. "Who brought this one in?"

"Hulk."

Hulk? thought Luka.

"Well *done*, Hulk," crowed the boy. "He's so cheeky and stubborn. There *is* a third option—one each of my Lost Boys have taken."

He blocked out the sun, and Luka saw him properly for the first time.

He wasn't wearing a crown. It was a mask—an old welder's mask, cut to form a familiar shape.

"Batman?" said Luka.

"Batman," said the boy, nodding. The rusting cowl covered his eyes and head, exposing his pale mouth and chin, and the thin scar that split his lips. Above his leather jacket he wore a torn choirboy's collar, long since dark with grime. "The Dark Knight," he whispered, "controls the darkness. He controls the city. He controls his enemies. This church, this neighborhood, this Bellum City—this is *my* kingdom. I am the Junkyard Knight."

Luka peered into the shadows. Other masks lurked among the towers of broken junk: Iron Man, Dennis the Menace, a dead president, and Luka's captor, Hulk—green plastic forehead held fast with tape.

"The Government locked my father away," said the Junkyard Knight, voice slipping into an incantatory rhythm. "Because he would not fight their War, they called him a deserter, and they threw away the key. He died in their cells a broken man—a lonely man. Now they want iron, and what they want they shall not have. We are the Lost Boys, Luka! We take the iron that would fight the War that killed our fathers and mothers! We are the Lost Boys!" The Lost Boys cheered and stamped their feet.

Luka thought of his own father—a noncombatant, a *medic*—crushed by the War's machine.

The Junkyard Knight pushed him in the chest, knocking him to the ground.

The Lost Boys whooped and howled.

"We swore the oath!" roared the Junkyard Knight, bright spit bursting from his mouth. He placed a foot on either side of Luka's ribs, eyes burning down at him. "We swore it! We are the Lost Boys!"

"*We are the Lost Boys! We are the Lost Boys!*" chanted the gang, dragging their feet through metal shards as they closed in on Luka.

The Junkyard Knight slid to his knees and grabbed Luka's head.

Luka met his wild black eyes and sensed madness whirring in the boy's mind, like a top spinning on its edge.

The Junkyard Knight pulled him closer, his breath seething on Luka's skin as the sun flickered behind him.

"Will you swear it, too?" he hissed. "Will you join us? Will you swear the oath and make the mark?"

He thrust the back of his hand in Luka's face, a red, swollen, stinking wound stretched across it.

"Will you make the cut and add your blood to ours?" screamed the Junkyard Knight.

"Where's my damn dog?" said Luka, panic, fear, and anger swelling in his belly.

"Forget the dog." The Junkyard Knight laughed, licking his lips. "Join us and we'll help you cook him! It'll be a feast! The greatest feast there ever was!"

He held a little brass key to the light, then slipped it into his breast pocket.

"We're going to lock the doors now. You're stuck

here. So why not shed blood with us? We bleed together! We loot together! We *die* together!" He threw back his head and howled like a wolf. "Join us, Luka! Lose yourself with us!"

Luka stared at the Junkyard Knight's dirty wound, at the masked ranks of the Lost Boys—and at their towers of looted scrap.

Ellie said I need iron, he thought. *Where else could I find this much of it?*

He opened his mouth to consent, to give himself to the boys' madness. But he saw in his mind Elena's face, her eyes wounded and wet, and he felt something snap inside him.

"I am *not* dishonorable."

The Junkyard Knight blinked.

"I can't hear you, child," he said, leaning closer.

"I'm not dishonorable. I'll never join you," said Luka, pushing the Junkyard Knight in the chest and clenching his fists, then louder, shouting into the boy's rusted face: "*Never!*"

Black eyes flared up at him. "Then we will *break* you! Lost Boys—get him!"

Luka scrambled backward on his hands, his weak leg sliding in the dirt, as the masks closed in around him, baseball bats appearing in white-knuckled fists.

The Junkyard Knight, smiling, raised his arms to the sky.

And the church exploded.

15

A blinding flash of thick white smoke filled the church, stinging Luka's eyeballs and filling his ears with a shrill whine.

Direct hit, he thought. *No sirens, no warning—I'm dead, just like all the empty houses and their soggy ghosts. Oh, Ellie. I'm sorry.*

Ellie.

As he thought her name, other sounds came to him: shouting, swearing, scuffling feet. Metal crashing to the ground.

Luka blinked.

Figures appeared in the smoke. Carrying baseball bats.

I'm not dead, he thought. Then: *I need to move.*

Pulling himself to his feet and swaying at the lightness in his head, he ran, dragging his weak leg behind him and pushing a pumpkin-masked Lost Boy out of the way as a brick zipped through the smoke and flew past his head.

"What are you waiting for?" shouted the Junkyard Knight. "He's getting away!"

"Hugo!" shouted Luka, running between the towers. "Hugo! Where are you?"

Another brick smashed to the ground behind him and rolled through his feet. He ran faster, blinking through the cloud of white as he scanned for an exit.

I've been here a hundred times, he thought. *I know this place!*

"Hugo!"

He reached the wall as another brick smashed against it. Rolling away, he threw a puff of smoke from the concealed pocket in his sleeve and ducked through it, blindly running his hands over the tangled thatch of objects piled in the church's pews. Coat hangers. Bike wheels. Spades. Tools.

"Iron," he whispered, pulling a giant spanner free and giving it a practice swing.

"He can't have gone far!" screamed the Junkyard Knight. "He'll need to get past us if he wants to escape!"

Luka rose from his hiding place, the stained glass light dappling the smoke behind him.

"Hugo!"

The dog appeared beside him, almost knocking him over.

"There he is! Get them!" roared the Junkyard Knight, pointing through the parting smoke.

Hugo bared his teeth and lunged forward, snarling. The Lost Boys hesitated—just for a second.

"Come on!" shouted Luka, grabbing Hugo's collar.

The big dog flew forward, white teeth snapping,

and Luka pushed through the wall of bodies. Spotting a stack of smashed TVs as he dashed through the aisles, he gave the bottom one a good pull and sent them all tumbling behind him.

The Junkyard Knight wailed.

Luka heaved himself onto a pile of stained and broken kitchen appliances beside the door, which fell with a glorious crash behind him. He ran into the daylight, Hugo at his heels.

The ruined neighborhood loomed around him, its bomb-damaged houses jagged against the bright sky. Luka sprinted through dug-out gardens and over broken fences, all the while expecting bricks to rain down around his head. But there was only silence.

He whistled and Hugo turned, his eager face cocked. "Just wait a minute," Luka gasped. "There's no one coming."

He looked back. The Lost Boys had the church's windows boarded up and blacked out. The only sign of life was the thin white smoke leaking from the spire.

"Was that a smoke grenade?" Luka asked Hugo, ruffling the dog's ears as he pressed his nose into his stomach. "I thought it was a raid, and I thought you were—"

His wrist scraped against something sharp on the dog's collar. He parted the fur. A cable tie—cut neatly in two.

"They had you tied up," Luka whispered as Hugo

licked his ear. "So who cut you free?" He looked back at the church. A great screech of falling metal rang through the boarded windows. Hugo barked.

"Yeah, I don't think I'll go back to find out," Luka told the dog, turning and running for home, his weak leg growling painfully, his path shadowed by a bus filled with slumped soldiers home on leave.

"That's a fine dog," said a Sergeant as she stepped wearily onto the pavement outside Luka's house. Hugo, hearing the praise, wagged his tail and leaned on the woman's legs.

"Thank you," said Luka.

She tipped her cap as she moved off. "Friends for life, they are. He'll look after you."

Luka ruffled Hugo's ears and threw open his front door, climbing the stairs as fast as his leg would allow.

Spanner clutched to his chest, he fell onto his bed, tension and fear rolling around his skull as he thought of Elena and Hazel, of the Junkyard Knight and the Lost Boys, and of the faeries who'd marked his house. Slowly, painfully, his whole body filled with a molten guilt that settled, heavy and hard, in his stomach.

He imagined reaching inside himself and scooping out that guilt in hot, stinking handfuls, ridding himself of its weight, leaving him light and happy and *free*, free of this terrible situation.

The front door slammed. Footsteps thundered on the stairs.

Luka opened his eyes.

Hazel's face was hovering, upside down, above him.

"You look terrible, Rake." He grinned. "How about that sandwich?"

16

Elena leaned on the broom, weightless in her boots, feeling as though the air itself was pressing like an underwater squeeze on her temples and lungs.

"Come on, girls!" shouted Little John, spitting onto the floor between his boots. "You're not being kept for free—you need to earn your keep here!"

"What are you doing?" hissed Stephanie, the girl from the bunk above.

"I'm . . . nothing," Elena managed.

She pushed the broom, once—then fell on top of it. Her movements were languid and slow; even the connection of her skull against the concrete floor felt distant and soft.

"Hoi!" shouted Little John, as the other girls dropped their work and rushed to Elena's side. "Get back to work, you lot!"

He stood over Elena and sniffed. "What's wrong with her?"

"She's fainted," said Stephanie. "*Look* at her! She's not well!"

"Faking it," growled Little John. He stuck a thumb into his nose and rolled what he found along his thumb. "She's smiling."

"I think she's unconscious," said another girl. "My mum's a doctor."

"And that makes *you* a doctor, does it? Get back to sweeping that floor—we've got two hundred sheep arriving in ten minutes, and this place needs to be clean before they get here!"

He nudged Elena with his boot.

The steel in his toecap surged through her and she cried out, the heat of the iron burning through her ribs and into her guts.

"See?" said Little John. "Faking it. She can go to the dorm. See how long her 'illness' lasts when she doesn't get dinner."

"If she's not, well she *needs* her—"

"Back to work!" roared Little John, spittle flying from his solitary brown tooth.

He carried Elena through the wrought iron gates, oblivious to the sparks that flew invisibly between the metal and the unconscious girl as the curse of the broken pact began to wring her in its grip, and she slipped ever deeper into the fairfolks' ancient, terrifying world.

17

"Well, what would you have done differently?" said Luka, pacing back and forth across the kitchen.

"I don't know," said Hazel, picking a seed from his teeth. "Burned it down?"

Luka stopped and cocked his head.

"You'd burn a church?"

"'S'not a church anymore, though, is it? It's a warehouse stuffed to the gills with the most valuable material in the world. Scrap metal's worth more than gold."

"I still can't get used to that," said Max. Hazel nodded.

"Can't build fighter jets out of gold," he said. "That's all that matters just now."

Luka pressed his knuckles into his eyes.

"So you'd have burned down the church. With what, exactly?"

Hazel looked surprised. "You don't carry kindling?"

"Who carries . . . Oh, never mind—"

"Smart people carry kindling," said Hazel, lifting a little pouch from one of his pockets. "Right, Muscles?"

"Just you, bro," said Max, cradling Hugo's head in his lap. "Just you."

Luka watched his dog settle under the evacuee's big hands. Max's eyes closed as he tousled Hugo's ears, and Luka thought he saw the glimmer of tears.

"Take a load off," said Hazel, leaning back in his chair.

"What?"

"Sit down, Rake."

Luka sat beside them at the kitchen table, where a loaf of bread sat beside a pot of butter.

"Makes sense these kids are in the old church," said Hazel. He pursed his lips. "Lots of space, and everything around there's been bombed out. Smart lad, this Batman fellow."

"He's not Batman," said Luka. "He's an idiot in a mask. He's made himself, like, a throne out of rubbish and—"

"*Cool.*"

"No, not cool! And he calls himself the Junkyard Knight, his gang is called the Lost Boys—"

Hazel laughed. "Like *Peter Pan?*"

"More like a horror movie. This is *serious*, I was nearly—"

"I like horror movies," said Max, blinking as though coming to.

"This is not a movie!" shouted Luka, slamming his fists on the table. "They were going to kill me just because *he* told them to!"

Hazel took hold of Luka's shoulders and squeezed.

"Luka," he said, his face serious, "I hear you. I know this is important to you, and I want you to listen to me, right now: we could totally fit a throne in our room, we just need to get rid of your bed and—"

"We are not getting a throne," Luka interrupted. He frowned. "And what do you mean get rid of *my* bed? It's *my* room!"

Hazel hopped onto the windowsill and adjusted a complicated series of dials he'd fixed to the glass.

"There's no *I* in *team,* Rake, but there is one in *buddies*. And that's us now; we're house buddies!"

"What do you make of this?" said Luka, ignoring Hazel and opening his fist.

"What's that?" said Max.

"It's a cable tie. It's how they'd tied Hugo up."

"So?"

"So, I didn't cut this!" said Luka, buttering another slice of bread. "There was a big flash of light and a load of smoke, then Hugo came to me, which means someone else cut him free."

Hazel held up the cable tie and produced a magnifying glass from one of his pockets.

"Big flash and smoke?" he said.

"Yeah. I thought it was a raid."

"Smoke grenade, I'd say."

"I figured that much out, Hazel, thanks. I'm not a complete idiot."

Max coughed.

"Smoke grenades are pretty decent tech. Tough to get hold of, for most people," said Hazel, taking the cable tie from Luka. "This is a clean cut. Knife rather than scissors—you can see it's been pulled rather than snipped. Who's helping you?"

"I thought . . ." Luka felt his cheeks color as he swallowed. "With the fancy tech, I thought . . . you, maybe—"

Hazel laughed. "Gotcha—right after you grass me up to the Warden Squad and get me kicked out of my tower, I risk my life to save you?"

"Why so much with the Wardens?" said Max. "What have you done?"

"Well . . . my tower, remember my tower—the one Rake had me evicted from? Well, there was a lot of stuff in there."

"What kind of stuff?"

Hazel crouched on the worktop and waved his hands as though shooing a moth. "Oh, you know," he said lightly, "highly classified documentation, private addresses of senior Government officials, the blueprints for top-secret military research . . . that kind of thing."

"Why would you even *want* that stuff?" said Max.

Hazel looked at him, puzzled. "Because they don't want me to have it."

Max gave a sort of "fair enough" facial shrug and went back to scratching Hugo's ears.

"Look," said Luka, taking a deep breath. "I need to talk to you about something."

Hazel cupped his ear and swung his telescope toward Luka.

"You got more juicy detail about narrowly escaping certain death at the hands of a bunch of mad kids?" he said, grinning. "Cause I'll be honest, I'm into that."

"It's not funny," Luka said. "There's something else, worse than the Junkyard Knight and his stupid gang. Something . . . weird."

"Oh, I love weird!" said Hazel, clapping his hands. "Let me guess . . . you *prefer* cold pizza?"

Max raised an eyebrow at Luka. "Do you?"

"What? No, I—it's not about—"

"You don't think farts are funny?" said Hazel, leaning back with furrowed brows.

"Farts are always funny," said Max. "That's just a fact."

Hugo barked and wagged his tail.

"I know, I—stop! Just *listen!*" Luka took a deep breath and tried to form his strange, terrifying new knowledge into words.

"I need your help with something properly weird and properly scary. You have to believe me, right? I wouldn't have before . . . but now . . ." He closed his eyes. "I broke a promise to some faeries and now they're coming to kill us all."

18

The silence was broken by an explosion of laughter.

"Faeries?" said Max. *"Faeries?"*

"Yes," said Luka matter-of-factly. "I laughed at first, too. But now bloodthirsty, murderous faeries are coming in three nights' time, and they're going to rip out our tongues and stab us with pointy sticks."

"That's even weirder than the pizza thing," muttered Max, reaching for the bread.

Hazel leaned forward, his eyes sharp and clear. "What are you talking about, Rake?"

Luka took a deep breath. "My sister used to put out an offering for faeries. Milk and bread. And I made fun of her for it because it . . . it was stupid, you know? She made me promise to do it last night, and I almost did, but . . . I threw it away when the bombs started falling—the bombs that hit Max's house. They were *real*, and the offering seemed silly . . . It doesn't matter. So I didn't do it, and then this morning all the windows were broken and covered in blood." He rolled up the blind to reveal another jagged, bloodied crack. "That wasn't the raid—it was the faeries. Which means they're coming, here, and they're going to kill us all because *I* insulted them."

Max had been chewing bread during Luka's speech. He swallowed. "Faeries," he said again, flatly.

"Yes."

"Are going to kill us?"

"Ellie sent me some screenshots," said Luka. "Look—"

"Forward them," said Hazel, sliding a new-looking phone from his sleeve and typing quickly.

Notifications pinged on Luka's and Max's phone screens.

"How do you have my number?" said Max.

"I guessed it," said Hazel, wide-eyed with innocence.

"How could you—"

"Is this a group chat?" said Luka, swiping the alert. "For *us*?"

Hazel grinned. "See the name?" he said. "House Buddies!"

"We're not 'buddies,'" said Max. "He sold you out. And I'm only here because they've blown up my house. You're just a couple of cretins I've been stuck with."

"A cretin is just a friend you haven't met yet," said Hazel, buttering another slice of bread.

"Oh, we've *met*," said Max, with feeling. "You climbed into my bed and tried to feed me instant coffee."

"I feel like you're not taking me seriously," said

Luka. He forwarded Elena's screenshots to the new chat. "Here."

Hazel and Max read in silence, chewing thoughtfully.

"So?" said Max, a moment after Hazel had secreted his phone away again.

"*So?* 'Nothing will stop them.' 'Interest in human agony.' That doesn't worry you?"

"*You* worry me. Faeries aren't real, bro."

"And what about *that*?" shouted Luka, pointing to the handprint on the window.

"What about it?"

"You think I'm making that up?"

"Yeah."

Luka buried his face in his hands. "You *have* to believe me—I'm only telling you this because I have to. If I thought I could do this on my own . . . I wouldn't—"

"Oh my God," said Hazel, grabbing Max's hand. "It's asking for help."

Luka screwed up his face and flashed his coin over his knuckles. "Not *help* . . . exactly, just . . . Look—you said I'm dishonorable, and I'm not. This is a promise to my sister, and now we're all in danger because of me and I want to make it right. So I tried to find some iron. That's the only thing that will save the house, and save *us*, because they hate iron, it's like their kryptonite. Only—"

"The Government is taking it all away for the War," finished Hazel. "You really picked your moment to annoy the Netherworld, Rake. Everyone's looking for scrap now: Wardens, gangsters—everyone."

Luka nodded. "I went to the bombed-out houses, but—"

"They only leave the shells," said Max, his eyes clouding over as he stroked Hugo's chin. "Everything useful gets taken away."

"Right. But that kid, the Junkyard Knight; he's got a church full of scrap right here in the neighborhood. And they'll kill me if I go back alone. But we can get in there, because I've got this."

He flipped his coin, which caught the light as it spun, peaked, then fell neatly into his palm, which he opened to reveal a small brass key.

"*Nice,*" said Hazel. "Rake's got skills!"

"That's his?" said Max, taking a soft-looking carrot from the fridge.

Luka nodded. "When he was trying to make me swear his oath I pushed him in the chest. He didn't even notice it was gone. Nobody ever does."

"Nobody?" said Max.

"You tell me," said Luka, throwing the key in the air and clapping his hands together to catch it.

"What are you doing?"

Luka opened his hands to reveal Max's phone, which he tossed across the room.

"Skills," said Hazel again, laughing and kicking his heels.

"So, we can get in whenever we like," said Luka. "And I thought, since we're all in this together now—"

"*We?*" snorted Hazel. He leaped onto the worktop and began filling the kettle. "Two hours ago you told us to get out and never come back. Now you need our help? Rake the Dishonorable?"

"I . . ." Luka managed, fighting against the sting in his eyes. "I'm not . . . Look. It's the house that's marked. You're in the house. So they're coming for all of us."

"Just say it," said Hazel, grinning. "'Hazel'— 'Brains,' if you will—'you technological marvel. Muscles, you muscular, handsome, muscular boy—'"

"Don't say that," said Max. "I don't believe any of this."

"'—I need your help,'" finished Hazel. "'I need you to help me. *Help*.' It's okay, Rake—strong people ask for help. Help help help help—"

"All right!" said Luka, throwing up his hands. "Help me! *Please!* I can't do this on my own. All I did was look around some houses and I nearly got killed. And if I can't find a truckload of iron these faeries will destroy us—all of us. You have to help me. Please."

Hazel and Max shared a look.

"This is crazy," said Max.

"We'll help you, Rake," said Hazel, holding up a

hand to placate Max. "But first you have to admit we're house buddies."

"We're house buddies," said Luka, throwing back his head and staring at the ceiling, "We can be house buddies forever. I'll marry you. Both of you—whatever it takes."

They looked at each other in silence.

"So, what's happening?" said Max. "We're actually defending ourselves against . . . faeries?"

"Yes," said Hazel, pushing himself up from the table. "And we need to find as much iron as we possibly can. Faeries and other eldritch creatures can't stand iron—something about the magnetic properties, I assume—so if we barricade the house with it we should be all right."

Luka's mouth fell open. "You knew?" he said.

"Well, not at *first*—but if you think I didn't notice bloodstains on your windows then you really don't get it. I know what the world smells like an inch from the ground. I know what the park looks like from every stone in my tower. I know what sounds the birds make when there's a dog on the path, or when there's a Warden coming. I see what's in front of me, and I notice *everything*, Rake. So, I did some research. You're in big trouble. Spilling the offering on purpose seems like the worst thing you could have done. There's going to be a Reckoning three nights from the moment of the insult—that's when they'll take out your liver with a burning stick and—"

"You *believe* him?" said Max, his mouth full of carrot.

"Why did you let me go on and on if you already knew?" said Luka.

"I wanted to hear it from you," said Hazel simply. "Now, luckily for you couple of lemons, I have already devised a strategy."

"A strategy?"

"Yes. It's like . . . a plan for how to succeed. And you really need one."

"I did all right."

"By 'all right' do you mean nearly being torn apart by a group of feral kids in comic-book masks who've taken up residence in an abandoned church?"

"Yes," said Luka tersely. "And I got this." He clicked his fingers and appeared the spanner from his sleeve, holding it in front of him like a sword.

"What are you going to do? Mend a bike?"

"I don't know—it's iron, isn't it?" said Luka, throwing the spanner on the table. "Couldn't I . . . leave it on the doorstep or something?"

"Oooh," said Hazel, pursing his lips as though savoring a delicious meal. "*There's* your strategy."

"Why are we even having this conversation?" said Max, his mouth full of bread. "This is *crazy*."

"Crazy is relative, Muscles," said Hazel. "From

where I'm standing, this—" He cocked his ear, then adjusted a sleek device he'd hung from a cupboard door.

"What *is*—"

"Shh!"

"Hazel, you can't—"

"*Shhhhh!* Can't you hear that?"

A low growl started in Hugo's chest. Max slipped his hand through his collar.

"It's just the dog," he said.

Hazel waved his hands frantically and stepped onto the table.

"Can't you just walk on the floor?" said Luka. "You've got footprints on the placemats, man."

"They're here!" said Hazel, as his devices burst into shrill alarm. "I knew it—they're here!"

Before he could respond, Luka's feet vanished from under him, his head landing on the floor with a thump.

Max stood, pulling at Hugo's collar and knocking over his chair. "What the hell is *that*?"

"Aaaaaargh!" yelled Luka, as tiny hands clawed his weak leg. He spluttered and kicked, but the thing jumped onto his ribs and ran up his chest.

"Wait there!" shouted Hazel.

"What do you mean *wait*?" said Luka, swatting at his stomach and scrambling backward.

A man the size of a soda can rose up under his chin, his gleaming black eyes fixed on Luka's.

"Is that a—it's a—" said Max, falling onto his backside.

The faerie shook his long hair loose, the sound of his grinding teeth filling Luka's head like a needle scraped against his skull.

"Arrgh!" he shouted. "It's on me! It's—"

The faerie drew a tiny sparkling dagger and raised it over his head.

"AAAARRRRRGGGGHHH!" screamed Luka.

Hazel's hands thrust out with a *click*, and Luka felt the snap of cold steel around his wrist as the tiny man fell back.

"What have you done?" he said, rubbing the steel band on his wrist. "What did you put on me?"

"It worked!" said Hazel. He laughed and clapped his hands. "They're made of iron—and it worked!"

"Whoa," said Max.

Luka's eyes widened. He lifted his arm. "Hazel?"

The faerie swung from a length of chain, his tiny wrist clamped into the other end of a strange pair of handcuffs.

"*Hazel?*" Luka hissed. "*What have you done?*"

Jem, thrashing in fury, shook his porcelain fist and howled.

"Mab damn your big, fat eyes!" he roared. "I'll cut you! I'll cut you all!"

19

With Max gripping his shoulders and Hugo pulling on his sleeve, Luka dragged Jem, whose sharp hands gouged spaghetti-like strips from the floor, back into the house.

"How *dare* you!" roared the faerie. "Let me go this *instant* or I'll bite off your—"

"I thought iron made you weak?" said Luka, sweat shining on his brow.

Jem gnashed his teeth. "Weak*er*!" he shouted. "Without these things I'd have thrown you onto the damn moon!"

Luka clenched his fists. "I'm supposed to try to *beat* the faeries, and now I've got one stuck to my arm!"

"This is definitely a pickle," said Hazel.

"You think?"

"Well, yeah, like you said: you've got a faerie stuck to your—"

"I *know* it's a pickle, Hazel! Why do you even *have* these things?"

"What do you think I was doing while you were at the church? I told you, I did my research, Rake. And I know where to find stuff—even half-human, half-faerie handcuffs."

"And where is that?" said Max.

"Where you get all the good, occulty stuff—the Necropolis," said Hazel, as though it was the most obvious thing in the world.

Luka closed his eyes. "The *crypts*? Oh, God, that's it, get them off me."

Hazel and Max shared a look as Jem hammered furiously at his handcuffs.

"I'm not sure that's a good idea," said Max.

Jem pulled the chain, hard, so that Luka dropped to his knees.

"Hey!" he shouted.

"Hay is for horses, biggun!" Jem spat.

"Do you have to be so loud?" said Max.

"I can be plenty loud when I want to be!" screamed Jem, staring at his bound wrist. "Aaaaaargh!"

"Why isn't it attacking me?" shouted Luka over the noise of Jem biting his iron bracelet then falling, screaming, to his knees.

The faerie cocked his head. *"It?"*

"He?" Luka tried, backing away as the faerie climbed his chest, Hugo barking in circles around them.

"Bloody well right, *he!*" screamed Jem.

"Those handcuffs are made of iron," said Hazel. "Like, *old* iron. He can't do anything if they're sitting on Luka's skin, right?"

"You think you're so clever, don't you, boy?"

shouted Jem, drawing a pair of knives from his coat. "Maybe I'll cut you up right now, eh? What d'you think of that?"

Max stepped back—but Luka lowered his face to Jem's.

"He's bluffing," he said. "He needs to wait three nights—that's what Ellie said."

Jem muttered something under his breath.

"That's true, isn't it? You can't do anything to us yet?"

"I can if I want," said Jem, pulling at his leather collar.

Smoke was spilling from his cuffs.

"What's happening to his eyes?" said Max.

"What about my eyes?" said Jem.

Hazel knelt beside the faerie. "They're going pink. You feeling the heat?"

"No," said Jem. His eyes flared crimson. More smoke poured from under his suit.

"Liar, liar, pants on fire," said Luka. "He's burning up!"

"Oh, all right!" said Jem, unzipping his jacket with a burst of steam and fanning his face. "Yes, that's the *law*, unless . . . But they wouldn't do that, even if . . . Yes, that's the bloody law. Are you happy?"

Luka could feel the heat radiating from the faerie's skin.

"What happened there?" he said. "Why did you go all red?"

Jem gritted his teeth. Beads of sweat formed on his brow and when he eventually spoke, it was as though every word was pulled from his mouth by red-hot tongs.

"I can't lie in your world," he hissed. "I burn if I lie."

"Oh my God," said Hazel. "So your pants *are* on fire?"

Jem thinned his lips and tried to look dignified. "Yes," he said. "My pants are indeed aflame."

"What else should we ask him?" said Max.

Hazel hopped onto the kitchen table. "Are you an assassin? Are you here to kill us?"

"No. I'm a watcher. A scout. I can't kill you until three moons have passed."

"How did you get here?" said Hazel.

"I move through the shadows of ancient things, from my world to yours."

"It has to be something old?" said Max.

"Yes," said Jem, starting to smolder again. "Aaaaa-part from toadstools. It doesn't matter how old a toad-stool is, a faerie can use its shadow to move between worlds."

"*Cool,*" said Hazel.

"What's your name?" said Luka.

"Jemas. People call me Jem."

"I'm Luka. This is Hazel, and that's Max."

Jem scowled, but said nothing.

Luka picked up the spanner and waved it over the faerie's head. "How come you can be near this if it's made of iron?"

Jem seemed to be thinking. Then he snarled, showing his charcoal-colored teeth.

"My suit," he said eventually.

"What about it?"

"It protects me from the poison."

"Like a diving suit?" said Luka.

Jem shrugged.

"Wait," said Luka. He swallowed and glanced at Hazel, who was frowning. "If the suit means iron doesn't affect you, then are we wasting our time trying to protect the house?"

Jem opened his mouth, then, as smoke began to ooze from under his suit, closed it.

"No," he growled through his teeth. "If you have sufficient iron around the entrances, the protection places a charm on your house. A barrier."

"The entrances?" said Luka. "You mean the doors?"

"And the windows. Do that, and even if we suit up so we can touch the iron, the building is protected."

"What about us?" said Max.

Jem took a sliver of roof tile from his pocket and bit into it with a *squeak*. His brow was low, his mouth hard. "If you're in the house at the time of Reckoning," he muttered, pushing Hugo's questing nose away, "you're protected, too."

"And then what?" asked Hazel.

Jem took another bite of slate.

"The Reckoning passes."

"And I'm free?" said Luka.

Jem paused a moment, then as though the word was sour in his mouth, said, "Yes." Luka almost melted onto the floor. "Oh, thank God!" he said. "For a second I—"

"But you'll never be able to do it," Jem added with a wicked grin. "The City's iron is almost gone. It's been spun into planes and bombs and bullets to feed your War. You bigguns have forgotten the old rules and devoted yourself to modern trinkets. This is a big house, and your crime was great. You'll never gather the iron you need!"

"Tell us more about the offering," said Hazel. "How does it work?"

Jem shrugged. "We do things around this house: tidying, cleaning, safekeeping from creatures of the darkness—"

"So, you really did tidy my sister's room?" said Luka, at the same time as Max said, "What kind of creatures?"

Jem finished his slate and began filling a clay pipe. "You don't want to know," he told Max, before turning to Luka. "Of course we tidied for her. That's the deal. We help, the humans make the offering. Everybody's happy playing along according to the rules. *That's* the pact. And now there'll be a Reckoning, because *you* broke that pact."

"I didn't mean—" Luka began.

Max and Hazel looked at him.

"Yeah," he finished. "I did. I'm sorry."

"Too late for that," said Jem, striking a match on the tabletop and sucking the flame into his pipe. "Vengeance is required. Otherwise, what's the point, you know? It's nothing personal."

"It is to me," said Luka. "They're my eyeballs."

Jem laughed. "That's a good one!" he said, blue smoke spilling between his teeth. "I'll tell them that—ha!"

Luka took a deep breath and palmed his coin. "What would you even do with my eyeballs?" he said, rubbing his wrist. The handcuffs were beginning to chafe.

Jem raised an eyebrow. "Eat them," he said. "Obviously."

"Look," said Hazel. "You might as well get used to the fact you're staying with us. We've trapped you in iron and we're not taking it off."

"You can suit yourselves there," said Jem. "More like me and worse are coming here tomorrow, and they're hungry. It doesn't matter what you do with me—I'm a servant of the cause, nothing more."

Luka leaned over him. "And you believe in that cause?" he said. "Even if it means killing us?"

Jem took another puff of his pipe. "Of course. I have to."

They sat for a moment—the boys, the dog, and the faerie—in silence.

"So what?" said Max. "We get as much iron as we can?"

"Knock yourselves out," said Jem.

Luka knelt beside him. "You have to listen to me! When I threw the offering, I didn't mean to insult anyone."

Jem stepped back. "You seek a bargain with me, boy?"

"No, I just—"

"There can be no *bargain*! You broke the pact—you made the insult. Spilling the offering on our own tree? It could hardly be more severe. If we let this insult pass unavenged, the lore will weaken and we will die. Your actions have put everyone in jeopardy: faerie, human. And your sister most of all."

Luka grabbed Jem's arm. "What about my sister?"

Jem shook him off. "We'll take her. You broke the promise, but it was hers to keep. She bore the mark of the fairfolk the second you broke the pact."

"What does that mean?"

"She'll be weakened by iron and will grow weaker every day until the moment of Reckoning, when she will be taken into the faerie world to live as our servant. In her place will be left a creature of our world—a hollow being with no heart and no soul—with only darkness where a soul should be."

"A changeling," whispered Hazel.

Jem nodded.

Max glanced at Luka, who fell back onto his haunches, twisting his weak leg painfully.

"So, there's nothing I can do?" he said.

"No," said Jem, but his skin began to smolder, and with a flash of anger, he added, "Get the iron! That's all you can do—just get the iron!"

Hugo sniffed around Jem's head, knocking his hat to the floor.

"Damned mutt!" he shouted. "I don't—"

The dog licked the faerie from toe to tip, his big tongue covering Jem's body like a glossy, pink sleeping bag.

Jem froze. Dog spit glistened on his face.

"What was that?" he said.

"He likes you," said Luka, scratching Hugo's ears. "I don't know why." Hugo barked.

"If that animal touches me again," said Jem, wiping his face clean, "I'll use his bones for jewelry."

Hugo barked and nosed Jem's stomach.

"Don't you—stop him!"

Luka snapped his fingers. Hugo sat, craning his neck to see if there was a treat coming.

"Cursed mutt!" shouted Jem. "I'll skin you for a waistcoat!"

Hugo barked and wagged his tail.

"Listen" said Luka, "once I get the iron, will Ellie—"

"Curse *you* and your infernal questions!" Jem roared, dragging Luka across the floor.

"Whoa!" shouted Luka, grabbing a table leg. "Why are you so *angry*?"

"You *insulted* us, boy! Do I need to explain it again?"

"But you're waiting for your Reckoning, right? Are faeries always in such bad moods?"

Jem narrowed his eyes. "If you must know," he said, "I dropped my sword as I was coming in to land."

Max's eyes widened.

"You can fly?"

"Do I *look* like I've got wings, biggun?"

"I don't know," said Max, shrugging. "This is all pretty new to me."

"I can charm corvids," Jem sighed. "It's considered a great skill," he added, with a touch of pride.

"Charm what?" said Luka.

"Like a crow or a magpie," said Hazel. "Right?"

Jem snorted. "A *magpie*? Oh, sure—look at me riding a magpie like a *farmyard* faerie!"

The human boys looked at each other.

"No serious faerie would ride a magpie," Jem said,

seeing their blank gazes. "Don't you know that?"

"Why would we?" said Luka. "We didn't believe in faeries until today."

"And there it is," said Jem bitterly. "The old ways are lost and the lore fades."

Luka felt the torrent of information washing him away, as though the faerie and the lore and the Reckoning and the iron had made a great wave that crashed through his mind. He reached for something solid, a strong rope that he could cling to—so he opened his chat with Ellie.

Seeing that his message still hadn't delivered, he thumbed through their last conversation. He clicked on the last screenshot she'd sent, its message of danger bright and clear.

Luka reread the last line again.

Perform an act of loyalty toward a faerie and you will find it repaid tenfold, he thought, turning to look out the window.

The Wardens who had swarmed Hazel's tower were gone.

"This sword is important to you?" he asked.

Jem took a moment to answer. "It was my father's sword," he said eventually, affectionate warmth spreading into his voice. "It's the one I was planning to use to slice you into cubes of meat."

Luka nodded.

"So, let's go and get it back."

20

"Are you *crazy*?" said Max.

"Yeah," said Hazel. "How are you going to hide the fact you're wearing a creature of the Netherworld as a bracelet?"

"What did you call me?" said Jem.

"He can hide in my sleeve."

Jem growled, and the room filled with the sound of his grinding teeth.

"*Hide* in your *sleeve*?"

"What else can we do?" said Luka, lifting him so they were eye to eye.

"*We?*" spat Jem, stamping his foot and knocking Luka to the ground. "There is no *we*, human! I am a member of the Seven Swords! I fought at the battle of Bobble Hill, and I will not be hidden from the world!"

"Look," said Luka, pressing his nose against the faerie's, his eyes almost crossing. "Do you want your sword or not?"

They stared each other out for five seconds . . . ten . . . fifteen . . .

Hazel started a drumroll on the kitchen table.

"All right!" shouted Jem. "But don't think I'm going to go any easier on you for this."

"That's cool," said Luka, who shrugged into his coat, waiting for Jem to climb into the sleeve first.

"Rake, why are you doing this? You *want* him to have his favorite boy-slicing sword?"

"And what if you get caught?" added Max.

"It's the right thing to do," said Luka, scratching Hugo's nose as he swung the door behind him.

Outside, the air was cold and sharp. Luka's breath billowed toward the sky, where the sun burned, sluggish and white, behind the clouds.

He turned to look at the house, running his eyes over the doors and the paint-peeled window frames.

"You're picturing where you'll put the iron, aren't you?" said Jem.

"No."

Jem chuckled. "It won't matter," he said. "I remember the old days, when humans were decent. Honest. Better. They'd put out an offering *every night*, sometimes, and we fattened ourselves on their chores. There was respect then. It was honorable."

Luka heard Hazel's voice again: *Rake the Dishonorable.*

"Where did you drop the sword?" he said.

"In that copse of trees—the raven banked too sharply, and it spilled from my belt."

"What does it look like?"

"It has a blade of obsidian, a rabbit's haunch guard,

a grip of goose gut, and a pommel hewn from the rock of the Midnight Quarry."

"Right," said Luka. "Cool, cool."

"It's a tiny sword, biggun. Keep your eyes open."

Luka climbed into the park, the distant City behind Hazel's taped-off tree belching smoke from its bomb-crater fires, sky-towers blinking in the distance. He could taste the familiar stink of burning buildings, a bitter coating on the back of his throat.

"People are still good," he said. "My sister's good. Ellie. She fed you, didn't she?"

Jem was silent for a moment. "She did," he said. "Until you broke her promise."

Luka felt a needle of shame pierce his heart. "I know," he said. "But I'm going to fix it."

Barrage balloon shadows bobbled across the park, and Luka vanished his coin over and over again, focusing on its edges against his tendons, forcing his mind into his fingertips as he spun the metal disk through his knuckles.

Ellie had always loved his tricks, laughing with him when he'd appear chocolate from behind her ear.

"Why are you moving so slowly?" said Jem.

"I'm keeping an eye out for Wardens."

"What's a Warden?"

"It's . . . someone who checks that everything is being done right. They tell people what to do."

"Like one of your Police people?"

"Sort of. But we only have them because of the War."

"A noble path," said Jem seriously. "They must be fine and dignified folk."

Luka thought about Mr. Stringer, the Domestic Warden who'd checked up on him and Ellie last time his mum went away—a renowned nose-picker who farted when he sneezed.

"Yes," he said. "They are."

"And you're afraid of these Wardens, are you?"

"They might take me into care, until my mum came back."

"Big risk to take, then, coming here."

Luka shrugged. "It was your dad's blade."

"So?"

"So, my dad's dead, too. And if I lost something he'd given me, then . . ."

Luka left the thought unfinished as he ducked into the cover of some bushes.

"How did you know my father had passed on?" said Jem after a moment.

"Because my dad's dead, too," Luka repeated. "No magic required." He crouched on the edge of the woods.

"What are you doing?" said Jem.

"Trying to listen."

"For what?"

Luka leaned back. "For anyone who might be around."

"Oh. *Oh*—you mean you can't see through the ground?"

"No. You mean you *can*?"

"Well, yes. It's a simple charm—I'll find a mole and borrow their senses. Would you like me to check these woods?"

"Yes, please," said Luka patiently.

Jem narrowed his eyes. "There is a life-form nearby."

Luka heard a splash. His heart rate quickened. "What *kind* of life-form?"

Jem narrowed his eyes again. "You would call it a frog."

Luka stood awkwardly and rubbed the feeling back into his weak leg. The frog blinked at him from a nearby puddle, then licked its eyeball.

"What would you call it?" said Luka.

"Well, it depends."

"On what?"

"On its name. This frog is called Steven."

"St—" said Luka. The frog burped, then hopped under some nettles. Luka shook his head. "Let's find your sword and get home."

They walked for a moment in silence, the *fiss* of the canopy washing over them.

"Are you all right in there?" said Luka, checking his phone: full signal, no texts.

"Oh, wonderful," replied Jem, voice muffled by the coat's thick fabric. "In all my life, I've never known such comfort."

"I'm doing my best. You should see how I'm having to walk so you don't swing about." He robot-shuffled over a puddle, arms locked to his sides.

"Your efforts are appreciated," said Jem. "I guarantee I'll remember this when I'm tearing out your fingernails."

"Do you have to talk constantly about how you're going to kill me?"

Jem thought for a moment. "Yes."

"Fine," said Luka. He began to swing his arms, like a soldier marching in a cartoon.

"Dammit, biggun!" shouted Jem, grabbing Luka's skin as hard as he could.

"Aaargh!" shouted Luka. He dropped to his weak knee. Jem reached out of the coat sleeve and grabbed hold of a tree root.

"Oh, please don't—" Luka grunted, pulling as hard as he could. "Jem? Let go—"

Jem tightened his grip and Luka felt himself lock onto the ground, immovable as a boulder.

"Jem . . ."

"Truce?" Jem grunted.

"Yes, yes! Just let—"

Jem let go.

Luka's energy was released in an instant and he leaped backward, cracking his head and rolling onto his back.

"You're welcome," chuckled the faerie.

"You did that on purpose," Luka muttered, scrambling to his feet.

"I absolutely did."

Luka froze. "Shh!"

"Don't you *dare* tell me to—"

"Listen!"

"To what?"

"Can't you hear that?"

"There are five humans approaching, yes."

Luka swung his cuff up to his face to get a good look at Jem. "You didn't think to *tell* me?"

Jem glared up at him.

"I didn't know I was supposed to," he muttered. "I'm not in charge of what's happening here, am I? I'm *your* prisoner, in case you'd forgotten."

Luka ducked behind a tree trunk. Seconds later he heard whispered voices, and peeked out to see five Lost Boys, each wearing a different superhero mask, tiptoeing along the path.

And slashing through the leaves, held between the leader's thumb and forefinger, was a tiny blade that was dazzlingly bright and glowingly sharp. It was obviously—could only have been—Jem's sword.

"It's them," he whispered. "And they've got your dad's sword."

"You mean those idiots in the old church? I know. I can smell them."

"How did—" Luka's eyes widened. "It was *you*, wasn't it?"

"Me what?" Jem looked away.

"You set Hugo free and set off the smoke grenade?"

"Well, yes. You're *our* quarry."

"But you saved me. Like, they were going to kill me."

"All fine and good," said Jem, inspecting his fingernails. "But while you must be punished, and it must be painful and unpleasant—it should be *us*, the fairfolk, causing that pain. Nobody else gets a slice of the pie, as it were."

"You saved my life," said Luka. "Thank you."

Jem was silent for a moment. "It wasn't a big deal," he said. "Let's away—there are five of them and one of you. My sword is lost."

Luka thought of himself fleeing through the church, and the precious seconds Jem had bought him. "Not today," he said.

And stepped onto the path.

21

Little John dropped Elena on her bunk and stood back, searching his nostrils with a thick, grubby thumb. "You think you're the first one to try this?" he said. "You think, after all the little City rats we've processed, you're the first one to think illness will get you out of your chores?"

He spat, and the sawdust leaped from the floor.

Ellie blinked. "I'm not—"

"Not faking?" Little John shrugged and brushed some blood from his coat. "We'll find out soon enough. Either you get better, or you don't. If you don't, you were telling the truth. And if you do . . . we'll find another role for you. Butchery, maybe. Make sure you think twice before pulling this again."

"Sir," said Elena, "I swear, I'm—"

"In the meantime, no food, no water. You earn those things here, same as everyone else."

Elena felt the sharp, hot pull of the iron in his boots and wretched, covering her mouth to stop the vomit. Closing her eyes, she felt the nails in the ceiling—their exposed tips sharp and rusted—pointing like accusatory fingers toward her, and she let out a sob.

"I don't know what's wrong," she said. "I can't stay awake, it's like—"

"Save it," snapped Little John. He grinned, showing his big brown tooth. "I don't care. You work, or you don't. That's it. And if you don't . . ." He licked his tooth and sniffed. "Think it over," he said, stomping down the stairs, each thud of his feet drilling through Elena's aching bones, her empty stomach spinning with a strange, sickly emptiness.

"Luka," she whispered. "What have you done?"

22

The Lost Boys froze, then straightened their shoulders.

"Little Luka?" the leader said, grin audible behind his Ninja Turtles mask. "You did some damage to our HQ, you know."

"Good," said Luka. "Who are you?"

The boy preened, one dark-skinned hand on his bat, the other clutching his lapel. "Shawn. I'm the Knight's second-in-command. Oh, he *will* be pleased! He's looking for you, you know."

"I'm right here," said Luka. "Now, give me that back."

Shawn looked at the sword. "*This*? This is yours? Playing with dolls, are we?"

"A *doll*?" growled Jem, quiet enough for only Luka to hear.

"Tell you what," said one of the other Lost Boys. "Come over here and get it."

"They are five and you are one," said Jem. "This is an impossible task."

Luka looked at the masks, and the bats in their hands. "But it's the right thing to do," he said, and ran forward.

An enormous thunderclap sounded overhead,

followed by the screech of tearing metal whistling through the air.

"What's going—" Jem began.

"It's a raid!" screamed Luka.

Another explosion sounded nearby, and the ground shook as a jet screamed over the trees.

The Lost Boys ran at him, waving their clubs. He felt Jem squeeze his arm and stumbled as another blast shook the ground. The raid siren began: shrill, electronic pips that pierced the ears and sped the blood.

He climbed to his feet, squared himself to face the onslaught of advancing Lost Boys, his fists clenching against his sides. When they reached him, he swung—missed—ducked under Shawn's flailing club and, as the Lost Boy stumbled, kicked him as hard as he could.

"Aargh!" yelled Shawn, straightening up and clutching his backside. "You'll regret that, you little—" He punched Luka's left eye, hard, dropping him to his knees. "Ready, boys?" he shouted. "Get him!"

Jem emerged from Luka's sleeve as the Lost Boys closed in. The faerie took Luka's forearm and pulled him to his feet, swinging and leaping and driving Luka's fist into bellies and chins and knees so that it appeared Luka himself was meting out a whirlwind of balletic vengeance: a series of blows and leaps worthy of a martial arts master, taking him high into the air and between the swinging bats of the Lost Boys with microscopic precision, striking out as he went.

And then he stopped so suddenly that he fell to his knees, twisting his weak leg beneath him. "What was that?" he said, breathless.

Jem climbed onto his shoulder and cracked his knuckles. "Get the sword," he said.

Luka stepped over the fallen shapes of the Lost Boys. The whole attack had lasted only seconds, but every one of his assailants was curled on the ground, clutching their injured parts and throwing up their hands to hide their tears.

Luka stood on Shawn's fingers and plucked the sword from his grip.

"Leave me alone," he said. "All right?"

The boy's chest was heaving, spit rattling between his teeth. "The Knight will get you," he hissed. "The Junkyard Knight will never be defeated."

"We'll see," said Luka. He handed the faerie scout his sword.

Jem sheathed the blade and released a satisfied sigh. "I'm still going to cut off your knees," he said. "When the Reckoning comes."

"At least you can do it with a sharp sword," Luka managed between frantic breaths.

Splashing past Steven the frog and climbing through his hedge, he checked his phone. It was dead. The networks had been shut off in the raid.

Oh, Ellie, he thought. *You wouldn't believe what I'm up to.*

23

Hazel and Max stood on the kitchen windowsill, watching the fresh fires burn through the rooftops.

"That message still hasn't delivered to Rake," said Hazel. "The network's still down."

"I thought you were off-grid?" said Max, folding a piece of cracked cheese into his mouth like a stick of gum.

Hazel grunted and shook his head. "Of *course* I am—my phone's connection runs through a proxy server on the other side of the world so they can't track it. But I still need the local networks."

They watched the sky for a moment in silence. Hugo sat between them and scratched his ears with his back leg.

"What else is there to eat?" said Max.

"Slim pickings, I'm afraid, even for those for whom the rations are . . . guidelines, rather than rules."

Max eyed Hazel sideways.

"Rules don't apply to you?"

"I know where to find things, Maximus."

"Like what?"

Hazel shrugged. "What do you want? You want

cheese? I can get you cheese. Bacon. Extra bread."

"What if I wanted more than a sandwich?"

Hazel laughed. "That's funny," he said. "I'm glad we're best friends forever now. BFFs, if you will."

Max shook his head. "Why did you believe Luka? About the faeries, I mean."

"Why *didn't* you?" said Hazel, adjusting a dial fixed to the glass and hopping onto the worktop. "Didn't you notice the blood on the broken windows?"

Max buttered another slice of bread. "No," he said, as though speaking through a pillow. "I was a bit distracted by the whole being-bombed-out thing."

Hazel nodded, then dribbled some coffee on his tongue. "Rake's not the type to make stuff up. And he's too stubborn to look stupid."

"But you *believed* him," said Max, swallowing. "Like, properly believed him."

Hazel cocked his head. "I lived in a ruined tower on the edge of Wildwood Park for a year. You know what it's like out there, at night? Everything is different at three in the morning: your problems are bigger, the shadows are darker. And stuff *moves*. I'm pretty sure I saw ghosts."

Max swallowed. "For real?"

Hazel nodded. "Maybe some of the things I saw were faeries, like Jem. It's not like you have trouble believing Rake now, do you?"

"No," said Max reluctantly. "But Luka was a right git when I got here and now it turns out he's cursed us both. I don't see why we should help him."

Hazel found a sausage down the side of the fridge and sniffed it cautiously. "If we can't protect the house in time, they'll scoop out *your* eyeballs, too." He slipped the sausage into his pocket, and a dial on the window spun shrilly. Hugo leaped at it, snapping his jaws.

"What's that?" said Max, his face white.

"That'll be our Rake coming home," said Hazel, vaulting onto the floor as the back door burst open.

Hugo jumped all over Luka as he ran into the kitchen, gasping for breath and peering through a swollen, purple eye.

"Somebody gave you a real shiner," said Max, swallowing. "Good."

"Be nice to your little brother," said Hazel.

"He is *not* my—"

"I went to the park," Luka managed, pushing Hugo away. He held Max's eyes for a moment—long enough to see the fear behind his aggressive front. "The Lost Boys showed up . . . just before the raid . . . Jem's sword . . . They'd found it—"

"The Junkyard Knight was here?" said Hazel. "No way! I'd love to meet him."

"Not him . . . his sidekick . . . Shawn . . . and four others . . ." Luka groaned as he slumped in a chair.

"I did tell him he was outmatched," said Jem, a

hint of admiration creeping into his tone. "But he kicked this Shawn right up his rear end."

Hazel's jaw dropped. "You?"

"Yes," said Luka, pointing to his closing eye. "So he hit me. Then it happened."

"What happened?" said Max.

"I did," said Jem, buffing his sharp little fingernails on his coat.

Luka told them the story, recovering his breath as he spoke, his pulse still hammering. He told them about rushing forward to get his shot in, only for the Lost Boys to close in around him with their bats . . . and Jem's strength flowing through him as he leaped and fought.

"It was like being a superhero," he finished. "Like, properly. I think I did a somersault."

"He was lucky there were no noble Wardens nearby," said Jem. "Just Steven."

"Steven?" said Max.

"The frog," said Luka, waving his hands. "Don't worry about it. The point is, I'm fine. Thanks to Jem."

They looked at the faerie—who blushed.

"It was merely a transactional exchange," he said, settling on Luka's shoulder and applying a whetstone to his father's sword. "You returned my blade to me, I made sure you remained solely the quarry of the fairfolk. Like I said, I'm still going to slice off your ears come the Reckoning."

Nobody spoke, and the kitchen filled with the sound of Jem's sharpening blade.

"O-*kay*," said Luka.

"Weird, huh?" said Hazel. "Why don't we break the tension by looking at my campaign maps?"

Luka blinked. "You've got *campaign* maps?"

"Of course. Don't you?"

"Well . . . no."

"Good heavens," said Hazel. "How do you people manage *anything*?"

He reached inside his boilersuit and began rummaging around the crotch.

"What are you—" Max managed, mouth curling in distaste.

"I'm on it, I'm on it, just"—Hazel gave a final stretch—"there!"

Luka caught the little cylinder as it flew toward him. "This is warmer than I hoped it'd be," he said, holding it between thumb and forefinger. Max leaned over as Luka unscrewed the cap and let the papers fall to the floor.

"Careful with those," said Hazel. "Painstakingly produced for every conceivable scenario: poison gas attack, nuclear bomb, natural gas explosion—"

"Okay. So, you've planned out what to do if we're attacked. How does this help *us*?"

"I'm getting to that!" said Hazel, rummaging through the pile. "Here—*these* are my treasure hunt maps. All the City depositories of anything you could possibly need: sugar, smoked meat, *un*smoked meat, circuit boards, electrical cable, power tools, soft cheese, hard cheese, *blue* cheese—"

"Why so much with the cheese?" said Max, holding a little map to the light.

"I like cheese. Didn't I say I could hook you up?"

"Why don't we just use our phones?" said Luka, unrolling another scroll.

Hazel slapped him on the back of the head. "Network's down for the raid, numbnuts. Besides, you think they can't track your phone? Right this second you'll be a little dot on some Government screen. You're probably already on a watchlist! Don't you get it? We need to go *off-grid*! Nobody can track us if we use these."

"But what if my sister needs me?"

"There's nothing we can do to help her right now, is there?"

Luka took a deep breath. "Just finding the iron and beating the faeries."

"Ha!" muttered Jem, turning his sword over.

"Right," said Hazel. "So there's nothing a text message can do we can't do ourselves."

"Network's out anyway," said Max.

"My muscular friend is right," said Hazel. "Just concentrate on finding the iron map, Rake."

"You have an iron map?" said Jem, leaning forward.

Hazel grinned at him. "Does that worry you?"

"Nope," said Jem, settling back against Luka's head and closing his eyes. Smoke began to rise from his collar. He clamped his hands to his neck.

"Ha!" said Luka. "He's lying!"

"I'm not!" shouted Jem, bright steam hissing between his fingers. "Argh!"

"Find that map, Hazel!"

"Is this it?" said Max.

Hazel grabbed the scroll and held it to the light. "If I remember correctly, we're looking at . . . yup! The scrapyard, train station, army depot . . . plus there's always the Church of the Lost Boys, and I happen to know the boy with the key . . ."

"No way," said Luka. "Not yet. They were already looking for me—and now we've beaten some of them up. They'll be on red alert."

"We need this by tomorrow night, Rake," Hazel reminded him.

"So we go there last. That way we'll know exactly how much we still need, right?"

"All right, fine. In that case, we start at the scrapyard, in the New Town. Then it's the—"

"The Necropolis?" said Max, peering over Hazel's shoulder. "You want us to steal metal from the *crypt*?"

"Ha!" barked Jem, fanning his face. "Scared, are we?"

"Hazel, how are we even going to get *into* these

places? There are Wardens everywhere. *And* soldiers!"

"So, we'll go at night," said Hazel, holding the map out of Jem's reach. *"Obviously."*

"Obviously," said Luka.

Max scrunched up his nose as Hazel dropped the little scroll into an iron tube and sealed it shut. "I'm not into this, man. It's not worth it."

"Fine," said Luka. "Stay here, then."

Hazel shook his head. "Let's not be hasty. We need as much iron as we can carry."

"So?"

"So how much can *you* carry, Rake?"

Luka's eyes narrowed. "I can carry plenty!" he snapped, his cheeks flushing.

Hazel held up his hands. "All right, but neither of us can carry as much as Mighty Man Muscles, can we?"

They all looked at Max.

"I eat lots of eggs," he said, his own cheeks coloring.

"And those eggs are going to save us all," said Hazel. "Look, if we don't get enough iron in time, the Reckoning will come, Elena will be taken into the faerie world, and our entire household will be slaughtered—you, me, and Rake."

Jem chuckled. Max growled and shot Luka a cold glare.

"Exactly," said Hazel. "We're all in this together: Hazel the Brains, Luka the Rake, and Maxi the Muscles."

"Muscles . . ." muttered Max, rolling his eyes.

"Those are our code names, right? Brains, Rake, and Muscles. We've got two nights to visit the places on this map and bring back all the iron we can carry—and not even two full nights. The Reckoning is at midnight tomorrow, right, Jem?"

"Right," Jem confirmed.

"As soon as we get the stuff home," Hazel went on, "we'll patch up the doors and windows with it. Easy."

They looked at each other in silence, the wail of sirens from the distant bomb sites needling into the room.

"So," said Luka, exhaling slowly, "your big plan is that the four of us—three boys and one faerie—break into highly guarded, strategically important military sites."

"Five of us," Hazel interrupted, holding up Hugo's ears.

Luka buried his face in his hands. "Sure," he said, his voice muffled, "why not take the dog? So, we're going to get into these places, with a dog, breaking about a hundred laws *as well as* the curfew?"

Hazel blinked slowly at him. "There's no way it's that many laws," he said, hanging a slice of bread in his teeth. "A couple of dozen at most."

Luka rubbed his eyes. "All right, a *bunch* of laws. Isn't that bad enough?"

"*You* went out to loot bomb sites this morning."

Jem started filling his pipe like it was a box of fresh popcorn.

"Only the stuff people really didn't want! You're talking about breaking *military* law—they'll probably shoot us!"

Max swallowed hard, the blood draining from his face. "I was supposed to be safe here," he said.

Hazel snorted. "They won't *shoot* us! They'll just send us to military prison."

"And that's a good thing?"

"Uh, obviously," said Hazel, with a get-this-guy shrug. "They're *much* nicer than normal prisons!"

"Ha!" barked Jem, striking a tiny match.

Luka flared his eyebrows and sucked his teeth. "All right, then. Assuming we manage to break into these places, assuming we manage to avoid security and cameras and *their* dogs *and* guns, assuming we actually get our hands on some of the most valuable, secure material in the whole City *and* manage to carry it back through the Warden-patrolled curfew in time for the Domestic Warden checking up on us at eight o'clock, how do we 'patch up' my house with it, exactly?"

"We weld it to the window frames. Strengthen the barriers, like. It's lucky I'm here, you know," Hazel added, licking some coffee from his palm. "You wouldn't stand a chance without me."

"We weld it?"

"Yes."

"And you've got that kit in your boilersuit, do you?" asked Max.

"Do you even have to ask?" grinned Hazel, twirling a welding rod in his fingers.

24

Nightfall came slowly.

Luka spent the long day listening to Max moving about in Elena's room: his feet heavy and slow as he arranged the furniture how he liked it, followed by silence as he read his yellowed book.

But even the silence pulled at Luka, as though the loose threads of his mind had snagged around the house.

Doing his best to ignore Jem's constant sharpening of weapons, as well as Hazel swinging in his hammock and fussing with tiny screwdrivers and a soldering iron, he chewed his bread and butter. It felt like paper in his mouth.

He tried not to think about the night ahead: about the darkness, the lawbreaking, or the ancient, angry faeries grinding sharp, black teeth in the shadows. If things went wrong at the scrapyard, they would be arrested and sent to rot in military prison where he, along with the faerie manacled to his wrist, would probably be subjected to relentless interrogation.

But even that sounded preferable to the alternative: his mother summoned back from duty to deal with him.

Luka shuddered.

Either way, the house would be defenseless when the Reckoning came. He imagined what it would feel like to have a sharpened stick pierce his organs, or have his tongue ripped from his mouth. But mostly he found himself thinking about Max and Hazel running across the scrapyard, while he fell behind and heaved painfully at his weak leg.

Eyes closed, gripping each second as it passed, he felt his stomach begin to boil again. He remembered the fear of having to give a talk at school, how the realization that it was *today* had crashed over him upon waking that morning, like a pail of water tipped on his skull after a blissful, empty sleep.

That had been before the War, before his dad had been sent to the front line, before Elena was evacuated, before his house had been invaded by Hazel and Max.

Before he had broken an ancient pact and been sentenced to a painful death by the Netherworld.

He checked his phone. The networks had been restored after the raid, but his messages to Elena still hadn't delivered.

"Come *on* . . ." he muttered, shaking his phone.

"Who you talking to, Rake?" said Hazel from the depths of his hammock.

"Nobody."

"Never a good sign, that." Hazel grinned, a crust

stuck cigar-like in the corner of his mouth. "At least talking to yourself makes sense."

"Talk to yourself a lot, do you?"

"Of course," said Hazel, unscrewing a section of blackened steel. "I'm often astounded by my wit and insight."

Luka rolled onto his side, pulling the chain connecting him and Jem and burping anxiously. "Charming," growled the faerie, his face lit by the bowl of his pipe.

"What's your insight about tonight, then?" Luka asked Hazel.

"It'll be easy." Hazel leaped from his hammock, then spun onto the wardrobe. "You sure your mum's not gonna come home?"

Luka shook his head. "She's gone for the rest of the week. Last time she went, she ended up staying longer than she was supposed to. Would you stop walking on the furniture?"

Hazel dropped onto the floor, then climbed onto Luka's headboard. "You feeling all right, Rakey?"

Luka frowned at Hazel's upside-down face, his skin lit a soft orange by the setting sun. "I'm a bit tense, to be honest, Hazel."

"How come? Everything's fine, isn't it?"

"Fine?" said Luka, sitting up and knocking Jem over.

"*Oy!*" shouted the faerie.

"How is *anything* fine?" Luka spat. "In the space of a day—one bloody day!—I've lost my sister, who I can't even speak to unless she climbs up the data mast—"

"She's on *that* island? Interesting . . ."

"—given up half my house to a giant boy who seems to hate me," Luka went on, "taken *you* in as some kind of crazy, airborne lodger, nearly been beaten to death *twice* by a group of feral kids in superhero masks, and—I don't know if you remember this— we're going to be murdered tomorrow by an army of tiny, angry faeries who're going to swap my sister for a changeling!"

"Darn tooting," said Jem, oiling his dagger.

Hazel pouted at Luka, then hopped onto the desk. "And whose fault's that?" he said.

"Mine!" said Luka, throwing his hands in the air. "And don't I know it!"

"But we're on it, aren't we? I thought you were feeling good about it—especially now you've got faerie super-strength."

"We are not a team, biggun," said Jem.

"It's not even that," said Luka, ignoring him. "What if I *can't* fix it? What if Elena never comes back, and it's all my fault? I don't care what happens to me anymore. I just want *her* to be safe. And I can't even talk to her."

Jem's whetstone slowed.

"Look, I know you're *really* worried about *me*," said Hazel. "But I'll be okay. Listen, the scrapyard's a good place to start. They'll have smaller bits we can just carry off."

"As opposed to what?"

Hazel furrowed his brow. "Well, we're going to have to unbolt sections of the train station to—"

"Whoa, whoa, whoa," said Luka, jumping to his feet. "We're going to take the train station apart? The *train station?*"

Hazel shrugged. "Yeah," he said. "Come on, Rake. Like, they don't leave spare rails lying around."

"How are we going to do that? What do you think it's made of? Lego?"

"No," said Hazel, settling on the floor and unzipping a duffel bag. "It's made of *i-r-o-n*. You can take that spanner you found in the church!"

"Oh my God," said Luka. "We're going to dismantle Central Station with a spanner." He covered his face with his hands, then jumped as his bedroom door opened.

Max loomed in the frame.

"Why is he crying?" he said.

"I'm not crying!" Luka snapped. "Close the door."

"Are we going now? It's dark."

"Not quite," said Hazel, glancing at the sky, still pink with the sun's final light. He lifted something from his bag and laid it on the floor.

"What's that?" said Luka.

"A Longitudinal Isolator," said Hazel. A screwdriver appeared between his fingers, and he set to tightening a tiny screw.

"Right," said Max. "You want to tell us any more than that, or—"

"You don't know about these?" said Hazel, eyes widening. "They're for listening through walls. Check it out."

Luka pressed the headphones into his ears while Hazel ran the pen over the floor.

"I don't hear anything!" shouted Luka.

Hazel laughed. "Yeah, you do—concentrate."

"Wait, is that . . . is that the kitchen clock?"

Hazel grinned. "You tell me. What else?"

"I can hear . . . Hugo! I can hear Hugo's feet twitching on the floor—he must be dreaming! This is amazing! Point it somewhere else!"

Hazel swung the pen in front of his mouth and blew on it.

"Ow!" said Luka, snatching off the headphones and rubbing his ears. "What good does this do us?"

"Well, Rake," said Hazel, as Max laughed, "if we're breaking in somewhere, it'll help to know if there's anyone around, won't it? This thing can hear a mouse sneeze at fifty paces. It'll stop us stumbling into a Warden's grabby arms."

"What else have you got?" said Max.

"Oh, lots of things," said Hazel dreamily. "I've got remote cameras, EMP bombs—"

"What's—" Luka began.

"Electromagnetic pulse," said Hazel. "It's like a bomb that only affects electronic stuff. Kills all the power. That's how I managed to avoid getting taken into City custody when I was bombed out. Set off one of these bad boys in the back of the Wardens' truck and the doors sprang open. By the time they'd pulled over, I was in the park, halfway up my tower."

"What did you use to hack into my gamer headphones?" said Luka, peering into the bag.

Hazel gently pried his fingers away. "*Hack* makes it sound like it was difficult. Home networks are so *easy*. Why do you think they ration and curfew your data and Wi-Fi? If I can get hold of it, so could the Enemy."

"What would your enemy do with that?" said Jem.

Hazel puffed out his cheeks, and raised his eyebrows. "Think about it: the banks are all online, medical records . . . everything. I bet your house has a central heating app, right?"

Luka cocked his head. "So?"

"So, if someone hacked into that app's server, they could turn everyone's heating off in the middle of winter, for as long as they wanted, and people would get ill and die. Or they could turn it all up to full blast and drain the power, so everyone loses their rations. If someone's online, they're vulnerable."

Luka thought of Hazel, cloistered in his tower, watching the City from a distance. "But not you, Mr. Off-Grid?"

Hazel grinned. "Right," he said. "It's the only way. No connections, no problems."

"These trinkets are a nonsense," said Jem.

Hazel stiffened. "How d'you figure that?"

The faerie sat forward, his alabaster skin glowing in the moonlight. "I can charm animals," he said. "Their bodies become as my own, my flesh becomes theirs, we think with a single mind. In these moments, we are one: I hear through their ears, see through their eyes, and feel through their skins."

"Can you fart through their butts?" said Hazel.

"The world opens itself to me," Jem carried on, ignoring him. "Whatever I need is there. There are no secrets."

"That's great," said Luka. "But we're not faeries. We need this stuff. Unless there's something you want to tell us."

Jem ground his teeth. "I told you in the woods that you are *our* quarry. If you're in danger, it's my duty to prevent another party claiming *our* prize."

"So, you're our bodyguard?" said Max.

Jem sniffed and looked through the bloody handprint at the night sky. "Until the Reckoning," he said.

Luka followed his gaze. The moon's pale sliver gleamed on the roof tiles of the blackout City, breaking through clouds like waves over the spires. The park was a sea of silver grass, shimmering like the surface of a pond. He turned automatically to Hazel's tree, now cordoned off with bright tape.

There were no Wardens to be seen, but that didn't mean they weren't lurking nearby.

His phone pinged, and he snatched at it.

Just the Government text—no signal, no Wi-Fi. The curfew had begun.

I'm fixing it, Ellie, he thought. *Don't worry.*

"Are we ready, then?" he said aloud, dropping his phone back in his pocket.

"Yes," said Max.

"Born ready," said Hazel.

Luka stood and waited for Jem to climb onto his shoulder. He saw their reflections in the glass and felt his pulse beat through his body.

"Then let's do this."

25

The streets were blue with shadow, and the sky hummed with the unseen rumble of drones. Luka tried to keep up as they ghosted along the walls, palming his coin and thinking about Elena. Bellum whispered in the distance, preparing for another night below towers and drones and hostile skies.

Hazel held up his hand and they ducked into a garden, huddling together with their knees in the vegetables. Footsteps swelled toward them, then passed, the telltale *click* of a Warden's boots fading gradually back toward the park.

Luka, his weak leg screaming at the awkward position, waited for Hazel's signal.

"Those are winter cherries, you know," said Max, gesturing at the bush Hugo was sniffing. "You should watch your dog doesn't eat them."

"They're poisonous?"

"Yup. Here." Max pulled Hugo away from the shining red berries and scratched his ears.

"You had a dog?"

Max nodded.

"I miss him. It was good having someone to look after."

"So look after Hugo," said Luka. "He likes you. He doesn't like everybody."

They looked around the garden. The ground at their feet was full of earthy vegetables, wintery beans and greens, and Luka tore off a spinach leaf to chew.

"Thief," Max whispered in his ear.

Luka thought he heard a faint smile.

"It'll grow back," he whispered.

Hugo barked as they moved on to the New Town's neat blocks and was shushed by a flurry of hands.

"Ready?" said Hazel, walking tightrope-style along a fence.

"Do we need *all* this stuff?" said Max, heaving the duffel bag back onto his shoulder. "You shouldn't have all this gear."

"Why not?"

"Because you can't even carry it yourself, that's why. You're a tiny little boy."

"First," said Hazel, "I'm a *big* boy. Look." He dropped to the sidewalk and rolled his top lip round his front teeth.

"What am I looking at?" said Luka, his hand in Hugo's collar. The big dog sniffed the air, his muscles tensed.

"My mustache," said Hazel, trying not to move his lips.

"Right."

"I've just started growing it, like."

"Uh-huh."

"That's not a mustache," said Max, shaking his head.

"I thought mustaches were made from hair that grows out of your face," said Jem. "Is this an imaginary thing?"

"I don't know," said Luka, running his thumb along Hazel's upper lip, as though checking for dust. "I think in ten years or so that could be a real cracker."

"Second," said Hazel, ignoring them and scanning the road ahead with his Longitudinal Isolator, "you never know what you'll need when you get there. Besides, it's only one bag."

"Which I have to carry," muttered Max.

"Tell you what," said Luka. "Heads, you carry the bag; tails, I'll do it."

"Fine."

Luka spun the coin and trapped it on the back of his hand. "Heads it is. Better luck next time."

Max groaned. "So, what's the plan?" he said.

"We follow Hazel," said Luka, crouching in the shadow of a tree.

"Brains," Hazel cut in, finger held up in warning as he waved his listening wand. "Code names, remember?"

Luka rolled his eyes, then sniffed. It was too cold to smell anything, though, and the air was sharp in his nose. "Fine. We follow *Brains*."

"Sounds good, doesn't it?" Hazel beamed. "Now, about our team name—"

"We need a *team* name, too?" growled Max.

"Obviously," said Hazel. "Has anyone ever heard of the Wild Hunt?"

"Nope," said Luka and Max together.

"How the lore is forgotten," muttered Jem. "The Wild Hunt! Neither of you knows it?"

Luka and Max glanced at each other.

Jem sighed. "The Wild Hunt has existed since the beginning of the world. Sometimes the huntsmen are elves, sometimes they are the dead, and sometimes they're *faeries*."

"Right," said Hazel, flattening himself against the side of a garage. "They ride across the sky. Hunting, together."

"Humans have seen the Hunt many times," said Jem, warmth creeping into his voice. "They said the huntsmen were bright-eyed and hideous, riding horses and goats, accompanied by jet-black hounds. Of course, when faeries hunt, we ride on rats and ravens. But no matter who rides, the humans hear the hunting horns and cower in their beds."

"What does that have to do with us?" said Max.

Hazel's eyes glittered. "Don't you get it? *We're* the huntsmen! We've got a hound and everything!"

Hugo barked.

"We can't be hunts*men* though," said Luka, shushing the dog.

"We're too young," agreed Max. "Even with mustaches."

"Fine, fine," said Hazel, rubbing his upper lip. "So we're the Hunts*boys*. The *Wild* Huntsboys."

"This is going to be a disaster," said Max as they ghosted between tenement blocks.

"I heartily concur," added Jem. "And I don't approve of you using the Hunt's name in this manner."

"Positive attitude, chaps," said Hazel. "Remember, there's a bag *inside* that bag, so we can carry our loot back without looking suspicious. *Too* suspicious, anyway."

Luka peered around the street. It was almost solidly black, the bushes and branches of the gardens swirling in the soft breeze like bubbles in ink. The darkness reduced their faces to skull-like masks. "How are we going to see anything in there without torches?"

"Muscles, the bag, please," said Hazel, rummaging in the pockets as Max lumbered over. "Here we go." He withdrew three pairs of goggles and swung them by their thick straps. "I'm afraid I don't have a faerie-sized pair."

"That's quite all right," said Jem. "I wouldn't dream of wearing them anyway."

Max looked suspiciously through the lenses. "We're going to swim when we get inside?" he said.

Hazel rolled his eyes. "These are *night-vision* goggles. We won't even *need* torches. Brains has it covered."

"I'm not sure you should have been allowed to choose your own code name," said Luka, slipping the goggles over his head. They were heavier than they looked, and cold against the soft skin around his eyes.

As soon as the clasp fastened there was an electrical *whirr* in his ear and the darkness around him glowed a fluorescent green. The world looked strange in night vision, all the textures and colors in the wrong place. Moonlight shadows loomed like boulders, and the curb edges merged with the road.

He turned to Hazel and Max. Every house around them was closed off behind blackout blinds, tiny slits of lights glowing at the edges of the windows.

"Here are your masks," Luka said.

"What you make these from? Tights?"

"Sport socks. *Clean* sport socks."

"I feel like a proper outlaw now," said Hazel, slipping his mask over his goggles. "Maybe we should rob a train on the way home."

"Maybe just focus on the one serious crime for tonight, eh?" said Max, moving his free hand in front of his face. "These eyeholes are uneven. How are we supposed to see?"

"Well, excuse me," said Luka, pulling on his own mask. "It's not like I make bandit masks every day.

And, by the way, it's more than *one* serious crime. They'll arrest us just for being out after curfew, *plus* breaking and entering—on Government property— theft, conspiracy to defraud the War Effort, reckless—"

"All right, all right," said Hazel. "What time is the Domestic Warden coming to check on you?"

"Eight o'clock. And me and Max *have* to be there. If they think we're not able to stay on our own, they'll take us into City custody until my mum gets back."

"Don't worry," said Jem. "The Reckoning will still take place."

Luka turned to him.

"You'll go after my mum?"

For the first time since he'd been handcuffed in the kitchen, Jem looked uneasy. "Whoever's in the house," he said after a moment.

"We have to get this done," said Luka. "We just have to."

"We've got an hour, Rake," said Hazel. "Easy."

Hazel pressed a couple of buttons on the side of his watch and pushed a Bluetooth headphone into his ear.

"What are you doing?" said Max.

"Shh! I'm checking the army scanners, seeing what they're up to."

"Can we hear?" said Luka.

Hazel glanced around the deserted street, shrugged, and pressed another button. Tiny voices hissed through his speaker.

Unit Three Alpha, continue on Stonemouth. Four Bravo—Cromarty. Four Juliet—Ferrous. All units be alert to—

Luka threw up his hands. "Well, that doesn't tell us anything, does it?"

Hazel frowned. "It tells us *everything*! You mean you don't . . . *oh*. Well, *Unit Three* means a patrol car, maximum of four Wardens. Four units are always trucks, maximum of *twenty* Wardens in the back, so keep your eyes peeled." His head shot up. "And here they come," he said, pointing.

"Life-forms." Jem nodded. "I could have told you that."

"Hide!" said Luka, grabbing Hugo's collar.

Crouching, sticking close together, they crept as quickly as they could along a row of houses and into a little cluster of trees, just as the convoy of blacked-out trucks rumbled into view, escorted by square-headed Wardens on electric motorbikes.

"Look," said Hazel.

Perched on the end of the truck, peering implacably from behind his frosted lenses, was the Trenchcoat they'd seen talking to the Wardens beside Hazel's tree.

"What's he doing there?" whispered Luka. "Isn't this just a normal patrol?"

"Apparently not."

"They're looking for you?" asked Max. "Like, really looking?"

Hazel fluttered his eyelashes. "Maybe."

"Why would they look for *you*?" said Jem.

"Well, some of this kit you're so down on is . . . pretty high spec."

"How high?" said Luka.

"Like army-research-lab high. A lot of it's quite experimental. *They* don't even know how to use it. I'm doing them a favor, really, getting it working so well."

Luka closed his eyes and took a deep breath. "You stole this stuff from the *army*?"

"Wonderful!" said Jem, throwing back his head.

"*Stole* is such a strong word," said Hazel, scanning the scrapyard through binoculars.

"But an accurate one?"

"Absolutely."

"Oh my God," said Luka, shaking his head.

Beyond the truck, among the roofs and driveways and neat vegetable patches, stood the scrapyard, its claw-handed crane silent and still, moonlight gleaming on its towers of battered steel.

Luka stared at it through the bright glow of his night-vision breath and watched the Wardens' truck turn a corner.

"Good chance they'll be around again when we get out," said Hazel, standing up. "Be quiet a second . . ." He held his hand to his ear.

"Why are you closing your eyes?" said Luka.

"Just . . . it's what people do in films. Right, they've gone."

"Again, I could tell you that," said Jem. "These trinkets are an affront to my skills."

"You'll be using those skills soon enough. We're the Huntsboys—the *Wild* Huntsboys. Nobody can handle us."

Luka looked at the Wild Huntsboys: Hazel and Max, noses squished flat by their sport-sock masks, standing behind Hugo, who was chewing his own foot so enthusiastically it was halfway down his throat. The big dog choked, crossed his eyes, sneezed, then started chewing his foot again.

"I don't think we're the first-string team you think we are," said Luka.

"Oh, don't say that," said Jem, trying and failing to suppress a snicker.

"Let's just go," said Hazel.

Luka led them across the street and squeezed through the first row of fencing. He wouldn't have been able to fit through it before the War, he thought. Rationing had made him lean.

The second fence was made of thick chain-link mesh. Hazel went to the duffel bag again and withdrew a long pair of wire cutters.

"Why do you even *have* those?" Luka whispered.

"How do you think I got all this other stuff?" Hazel whispered back.

Max cut out a square of metal.

"Best keep that," said Hazel. "Stick it in the bag." He scanned the darkness with the Longitudinal Isolator, then shook his head. "Nothing. Jem?"

"There are humans in there. But none close by."

"Good enough for me," said Hazel, and he disappeared into the scrapyard.

"You next," said Max.

Luka turned to Jem. "You'll be all right in here?"

The faerie pulled a bird-skull mask over his face. "So long as I'm suited up," he muttered.

"This is crazy, isn't it?" said Luka, glancing at Max.

"Yup. Hurry up."

Luka peered into the darkness behind the fence, belly bubbling so powerfully with anticipation that he felt everything else—fear, disbelief, self-doubt— evaporate, leaving only a clear vapor of knowing, *knowing*, that beyond this threshold was a new life, and the start of a transformation he could never undo.

Hugo nosed his ear.

Luka palmed his coin and slipped through the fence.

PART TWO

The appearance of the Wild Hunt is most common during times of war and is believed to foretell tragedy or suffering. Legend says that the Huntsmen wear frightening masks and that though each has his own particular strength—in bravery, resourcefulness, or cunning—it is only through their powers combined that they succeed in the Hunt for their eternal quarry.

The Wild Hunt in Popular Mythology, Chabon Lurtz

26

The scrapyard was quiet and still. Smashed cars and buses were stacked around them, the jagged steel of hoods and grills jutting like broken bones. Luka ran his hand along a silver Mercedes.

"This used to be such a fancy car. Now it's just bits of junk."

"Everything's just a bunch of parts stuck together, Rake," whispered Hazel. "When you think about it, you're just a bag of organs wrapped in meat."

"*Fragile* meat," added Jem.

"Yeah, yeah," said Luka. "Right, what should we—"

"Whoa, whoa, whoa!" whispered Hazel. He lifted the Longitudinal Isolator. "We've not brought this stuff for nothing, have we? There're security guards in here. With dogs." He pointed the isolator's pen into the darkness ahead of them and closed his eyes.

"Anything?" said Luka.

Hazel nodded.

"What?"

"You saying 'anything' and 'what.'"

Luka punched his arm. "I mean any—"

"I know, I know. There's a guard up there. Hundred yards away. Keep behind me."

The other Huntsboys nodded, then followed him into the darkness. Luka felt the remnants of ruined machines under the soles of his feet: pistons and springs and seat belts, dropped by the crane's jaws like bitten-off spaghetti.

"The guard is coming this way," Hazel whispered. "I think."

"You *think*?" said Max.

"Yeah. Hang on." Hazel rummaged in the duffel bag. "It was definitely in here."

Luka peered over his shoulder. "What was?"

"My visualizer. Aha!" He pulled a small, black leaf-blower-shaped thing from the bag and clicked it on.

"What does *that* do?" said Max.

"Look." A small screen on the thing's handle hummed into life, glowing with a mass of bright blobs.

"I still don't get it," whispered Max.

"Me neither," said Luka.

"Oh. Well, this is us, and *that* little dot"— Hazel tracked a pinprick of bright blue with his fingertip—"is the security guard. And *that's* his dog."

They watched the little dots glide across the screen.

"So it's like *Pac-Man*?" said Luka.

"No, it is *not* like . . ." Hazel paused. "It's a bit like *Pac-Man*, I suppose, yeah."

"Doesn't that moving light mean that the guard is coming this way?" said Jem.

"Yes!" hissed Hazel, pleased. "See, *Jem* gets it—they're coming right at us!"

"Right," said Luka. "Shouldn't we run away, then?"

"Oh, yeah," said Hazel, as they heard the first crunch of footsteps. "Wait!" he added, going to one of his pockets. "The dog—"

"What now?" whispered Luka, feeling the beginnings of panic as the footsteps drew closer. "Anti-dog technology?"

"Sort of," said Hazel, waggling a sausage at him. Max stifled a laugh.

Hugo licked his lips and sat obediently.

"Did you get that from my fridge?"

"It's *our* fridge, Rake." Hazel stuffed the sausage in the eye socket of a missing headlamp in the closest car.

Crouching, his heart beating so hard it felt like it was going to unravel, Luka shuffled across to the opposite wall of smashed cars, Hugo pulling back toward the hidden sausage. He felt suddenly exposed, the wind blowing down the pathway's little tunnel, and he tensed his muscles in anticipation of a grabbing hand or snapping jaw.

"Here he comes!" said Hazel, ducking into a shadow between Hazel and Max. Jem hunkered down against his head, and Luka was surprised to find reassurance in the faerie's weight.

He tightened his grip on Hugo's collar and peered out.

The security guard was a squat man with a squat man's walk, all swinging tummy and waggling baton. The dog—rather than the slavering hound Luka had imagined—was only a spaniel, but it leaped and snarled at the sausage in the headlamp. Hugo whined and pawed the ground.

"Hoi!" shouted the guard. "Is somebody there?"

The yard rang with the tinny sound of his dog's scrambling claws.

"Rake?" whispered Hazel.

"What?"

"Can you see the keys on that man's belt?"

Luka peered through his goggles at the guard's glowing image. A bright shape on his midsection caught the moonlight like a fishing lure.

"I think so."

Hazel grinned, then nudged Luka's shoulder. "It would really help if you could steal those," he said.

"What?" hissed Luka. "No way. We're already in, aren't we?"

"Yeah, but the best stuff will be next to the incinerator—which is behind that gate."

Max looked between them, his lips anxious and thin.

"Don't you have a lockpicking kit in this bag?" he whispered.

"Sure I do—but picking locks takes time. If you get those keys, we'll be in and out in two shakes of a faerie's finger."

Jem, moonlight bright on his bird-skull mask, rolled his eyes.

"I'm not a pickpocket, Hazel—" Luka began.

"Call me Brains!" hissed Hazel. "And you *are*—you took my flash drive this morning."

Luka turned to Max. "You think this is crazy, too, right?"

Max shrugged. "It's like he said, I guess—keys'll be faster than a lockpick."

Luka looked up at the stars, bright behind the looming scrap heaps. He thought about the earth spinning through space, about all the billions of lives that played out over its surface every single day, and wondered how *this* was happening to *him*.

"Fine," he said, handing Hugo's collar to Max and tiptoeing forward.

He felt, once again, open and exposed—the wind whipped the fabric of his jumper against his skin, and his muscles tensed with the flash of cold.

The spaniel was still scrabbling at the empty head-lamp, its whine disguising the crunch of Luka's feet.

"You can do this, you know," whispered Jem. "You've got fast hands."

"What is it, girl?" the guard said, leaning in and

shining his torch between the cars. "Is somebody there?"

Luka froze at the man's voice. *I'm going to get caught,* he thought. *He's going to turn around and shine that torch in my face, and that dog's going to tear out my throat.*

He took another slow step, crouching as he moved onto his weak knee, blanking out the pain that swelled into his hip, his outstretched hand inches away from the swinging keys.

And, just as his fingertip brushed the man's belt, he had another thought.

I'm covered in Hugo's fur.

The dog wheeled around, snarling, the sausage forgotten as the threat of another animal reached its brain.

"Whoa!" shouted the guard, striking his head on the overhang of a ruined pickup. He tugged the lead and shone the torch about, casting a pale disk over the deep shadows in the grime and steel. "Dammit, dog! There's nothing there!"

He stamped away, dragging the yelping spaniel and muttering under his breath.

Silence fell over the yard. Then came an amphibian chirp from the Huntsboys' hiding spot, followed by: "Rake?"

Luka unfolded from a puddle of gloom. Hugo

bounded over to him, running in a circle. "That was close."

Hazel and Max tumbled onto the path.

"You just disappeared!" said Max, admiration creeping into his voice.

Luka waved his hands, then plucked his coin from the air.

"The Great Maldini has his ways," he said, bowing.

Hazel laughed.

"Why didn't you answer my signal?"

"The animal noise?"

"Yeah," said Hazel. "This." He made the frog-like click again.

"You know, *Brains*, we should probably discuss call signals in advance. What do you think, Muscles?"

Max grinned sheepishly. "To be fair, I also thought you ran off like a big chicken."

"Never mind," said Luka.

"You got the keys then?" said Hazel, watching the guard's little dot disappear from the visualizer's screen.

Luka reached behind Hazel's ear and withdrew the key. "Easy peasy," he said.

"Rake!" said Hazel, clapping. "Isn't that great, Muscles?"

"Yeah," said Max, raising his eyebrows, "he actually did."

"You did well," said Jem. "For a human."

Luka looked down modestly.

"Remember," said Hazel, unlocking the incinerator gate. "Small pieces, and make sure they stick to your magnet first—there's no point in accidentally covering the house in tin." He tiptoed forward, only the yellow lights on his goggles visible in the darkness. Luka stumbled after him, tripping over car parts and torn machinery.

After twenty or so paces, Hazel held up his hand and crouched beside the gate, watching the visualizer. "He's gone. Do you know which key it is, Rake?"

"I was supposed to ask?"

"Good point." Hazel pulled out the loaded key ring and tried one. "Hang on—"

He tried another and another, moving each failed attempt to the other side of his thumb. "This guy's got more keys than a jailer," he muttered, sliding another doomed key into the lock.

"We're trying *not* to think about jail, Brains," said Luka.

Max shifted uncomfortably beside him.

"Only a couple to go."

High above them, the dinosaur-neck crane gave a juddering sigh, like a train coming to rest.

"It's always the last one, isn't it?" said Hazel, opening the lock with a shrill whine as rain began to fall. "Magnets up, Huntsboys." He pushed the gate inward on silent hinges, revealing the macerated scrap beyond: silvery dunes of torn steel, piled in undulating waves.

"This is more than we'd ever need," Luka said— and then the breath stopped in his throat.

"You should have asked *me*," said Jem, "instead of relying on these infernal devices."

There, right in the center of the yard with moonlight radiating from his rusted mask, stood the Junkyard Knight.

27

The nails had grown longer, Elena thought. Their crooked points were closer to her face, bearing down on her like slow, steady missiles. She tried to lift her arm, but it was stuck to the bed, exhaustion filling her veins like liquid lead.

"You should eat the broth," said Stephanie, pressing her open palm to Elena's forehead. "It's no wonder you can't move, with such an empty stomach. Eat something."

Elena moved her tongue against her teeth. "I tried," she said. "It came straight back up."

Stephanie sighed. "I need to get back to work. You're lucky, being so sick and all."

"Yeah," said Elena. "Sure."

She listened to Stephanie's feet vanishing on the stairs.

Not lucky, she thought. *Not lucky at all.*

She looked at her nails again, and thought about her old books. They said different things about the faeries, some speaking fearfully, others with excitement. Depending who you believed, the fairfolk were either misunderstood victims or bloodthirsty demons bent on the destruction of humankind. But they all agreed on one thing.

Iron *hurt* faeries.

Elena closed her eyes and reached out to the nails driven into the bunk above her head, allowed their chiming song—undetectable by human ears—to fill her.

She felt the air moving over their rusting surface, felt their iron glow as though burning hot, a projection of magic so ancient it seemed to come from the bones of the earth, both pulling and repelling so that she hung motionless, unable to move, empty of strength and losing the power to even breathe.

She began to retreat further in her mind, to the bolts in the bedframe and the nails in the floor, through the wrought iron beams in the dormitory walls and the pots and pans in the steamy kitchen below. Iron—ancient, terrible, and powerful—flowed through the old building as invisible torrents that charged, spiraled, and pulsed.

"No," she said, opening her eyes, trying to climb back into her human skin and gripping the bedsheets to feel something else, something of the world she knew, something that wasn't the pain that lived on the other side of her thoughts.

"Luka," she whispered. "Luka, you have to fix this. Help me, please!"

She looked at her phone's blank screen and then—
for the first time since she'd arrived in this place of
anger and pain—she wept. Softly at first, then uncon-
trollably, tears soaking into her hair as the iron flowed
toward her.

28

For a moment, nobody moved.

Hazel knelt where he was, hand in midair; Max held his half step into the yard. Hugo growled, hackles rising on his back. Luka's lungs felt flat and empty.

The Junkyard Knight relaxed his shoulders and walked forward, hands out as though amused to find himself caught in the rain.

"Luka," he said, his voice barely above a whisper. "Making a habit of showing up on our turf, aren't you? You were lucky this morning—not so lucky now, though!"

"What about Shawn?" said Luka. "How lucky was that?"

"He's fine." The Knight shrugged a bat from a holster on his back. "Looking forward to seeing you again."

All around them, masked figures were sliding down the glittering scrap with a soft metallic *hiss*, hands poised like surfers cresting a wave.

Raindrops spat from the Knight's bat as he pointed it toward the Huntsboys.

"Run?" Hazel whispered.

Without another word the Huntsboys parted, each darting in different directions into the darkness.

"Get them!" hissed the Junkyard Knight.

The assembled boys vanished like bugs under a kitchen light, and in a few seconds the yard had emptied into the narrow lanes between the towers.

Nobody shouted, nobody cried out. They just ran.

Luka darted down a narrow channel behind the furnace, slipping on a slick shingle of metal shavings and steadying himself on Hugo's shoulders.

"You need to think tactically," shouted Jem, climbing onto his shoulder.

"What? How?"

"There's more of them, isn't there?"

"How does that help?" Luka hissed through clenched teeth.

"Think! If there's more of them, then they're more likely to get caught by those guards. Right?"

Luka slipped again, plunged his magnet into the ground, and threw the scrap shards it attracted over his shoulder.

Jem glanced backward. "It'll take more than that," he said. "I thought you were a magician?"

"I am!" said Luka. He reached into his sleeve and unfurled a string of colored flags, looping the cord round a wing mirror and turning the corner to create a trip wire, before rolling through a gap in the mounds of junk. There was a cry, followed by the splash of someone falling to the ground.

"Better!" shouted Jem, his grin almost audible.

Ahead, Luka saw more Lost Boys waiting with bats raised, moonlight shining on their masks' fixed expressions. He changed direction, stumbling on his weak leg.

"We need to even the numbers," Luka said. "We need the guards."

"Good boy," said Jem, spinning a hubcap like a Frisbee behind them.

"Hey, Lost Boys!" Luka shouted, waving. "Over here!"

Everyone froze.

"What are you waiting for?" said Luka. "I'm right here! Come and get me!"

The Junkyard Knight stomped into view, Hazel's twisted arm in his grip. He held a finger to his lips and shook his head.

"Or what?" said Luka, as Jem slipped back into his sleeve. "What are you going to do? Help! *Help!*"

Hazel's mouth dropped open. He shook his head at Luka, his lips mouthing an impassioned *No!*

The Junkyard Knight gave another twist. Hazel dropped to one knee.

A guard dog barked in the distant yard, and a dim light appeared below the crane. The Junkyard Knight pointed at Luka and drew a finger across his throat.

Luka could see the glitter of his eyes inside the mask.

"Come on, then!" he shouted, throwing more scrap shards at the nearest Lost Boys. "Catch me!"

"Get him, for God's sake!" bellowed the Junkyard Knight, throwing Hazel to the ground. "Don't just stand there!"

"But you said—" started another boy, throwing an anxious glance toward the advancing torchlights.

"Never mind what I said! Just—"

But it was too late. His Lost Boys were fleeing, scrambling up the scrap dunes with deep, tinkling lunges and heaving themselves through a gap in the barbed wire.

The Junkyard Knight whirled about in desperation. "Don't—we can't let him—!"

Luka whistled.

The Junkyard Knight turned to face him.

Luka tried to breathe past the lump in his throat. "You staying?" he said.

The Junkyard Knight put his head to one side, his mouth twisting. He turned and watched his followers fleeing over the ramparts, then looked past Luka to the swinging torches and the eager whine of tight-leashed dogs.

"Next time," he said, rain bouncing from his outstretched bat. He spat a spray of rain and phlegm between his boots. *"Next time."*

Hugo barked after him as he turned and bounded up to the fence, swinging his legs up and through it in a single movement.

Hazel stumbled toward Luka, Max appearing at his shoulder.

"That was good thinking, Rake," he said. His eye was cut and swollen, his lip bleeding. "Apart from that, we're stuck here now."

"One thing at a time," said Luka, ducking into a shadow.

"Now what?" said Max. His arm was bleeding, and his jumper was torn.

"What happened to you?" said Jem, reemerging onto Luka's arm.

"Nothing. I happened to them."

"*Nice,*" said Jem, nodding approvingly. He was visibly sweating in the presence of so much iron.

"You okay?" Luka asked him.

Jem waved away his concern.

"I told you, I'm suited up." He dabbed under the bird skull with a tiny handkerchief. "But it still hurts."

Hazel pulled the duffel bag from Max's shoulder and started rummaging in a frenzy. "If I can find the EMP bomb, then—"

"No way," said Luka. "No bombs! I mean, we—"

"EMP!" said Hazel. "Electronics, remember? There's no fire or anything, it just means all their cameras and visualizers will stop working."

"Wait, they've got visualizers, too?"

"Well, yeah—where do you think I got mine?"

Luka's wind left him in a single, deflating gust.

"We're going to prison, aren't we?" he said.

The guards' hurried steps crunched closer, and the beams of their torches bounced over the Huntsboys' shoes.

"Oh, for Mab's sake . . ." said Jem, launching Luka toward the crane.

Hazel and Max sprinted away from the guards, Hugo barking upward as he ran, their eyes all fixed on Luka's scrambling form.

"Look at him go!" screamed Hazel.

"What are you doing?" Luka shouted, as Jem swung him up and over another pillar of steel. He felt the faerie's strength coursing through him, as though the handcuffs' iron chain was charged with electrical power. "We need to get out of here," Jem shouted, "and *apparently* I'm the only one with any notion of what to do!"

Together, they leaped onto a stack of flattened cars and ran *up* its side like it was a sidewalk.

Luka glanced down. Already they were forty feet in the air, and closing on the crane's distant cab. The City's blacked-out silhouette hummed before him, the lights of drones and sky-towers blinking through the clouds.

Jem kicked open the cab door, and Luka found his hands clasping and pulling the levers.

"Do you know how to work this?" he said, breathless and sweating. The guards' torches were swinging in his direction.

"Of *course* not!" said Jem. "Just push the buttons." He started madly jabbing at the control panel.

There was a mechanical roar of tearing steel as the crane swung on its axis, its huge arm smashing through a pile of junk and sending it flying through the night sky.

Lights flooded Luka's sensitive night vision and smashed through the yard as the crane's grabbing fist clanked open and thudded to the ground.

"Watch out!" shouted Luka, watching the other Huntsboys dive for cover. He saw Hazel and Max drop to their knees, wrapping Hugo in their arms.

The guards' torches had vanished in the blazing light and they stood, blinking, in a confused circle.

"Ready?" said Jem.

"I don't—aargh!" shouted Luka, as the faerie dragged him from the crane's cab and used his arms to abseil down its enormous cable.

"Hold on!" Jem shouted.

"Aaaaaaarrrrrrrghhh!" Luka screamed, the steel burning through his coat.

He landed beside Hazel and Max, did a forward roll, and got a lick in the face from Hugo.

"That was so cool!" shouted Hazel, clapping his hands.

"Run!" said Luka, pushing him forward.

The crane arm rose beside them, showering the yard with a waterfall of roaring metal.

"How is it still moving?" Luka yelled.

"I think we broke it!" Jem shouted back.

The guards, hands covering their heads, looked up as the Huntsboys leaped over them, their dogs snapping on the ends of their leads.

Luka grabbed a crooked fender beside the gate, his fingers slipping on the rain-soaked surface. "Grab some iron!" he shouted.

The other two reached down and lifted pieces of scrap as they ran: license plates and engine parts and lengths of pipe.

The crane arm smashed down once more in an explosion of shards, and a stack of flattened cars began to groan and lean like a wind-bent tree.

"*Run!*" screamed Luka, clutching a battered twist of exhaust pipe to his chest.

A chorus of car horns burped into the night behind them, like a gaggle of deflating geese, and the ruined cars tipped over in a cacophonous wave, smashing to the ground at the Huntsboys' frantic heels.

They fled down the streets, blackout shutters flying up as they passed, and dived into the safety of the park as the Wardens' truck screeched into view, the scrapyard lights blazing in the Trenchcoat's frosted eyes.

29

The kitchen door banged open, and the Wild Hunts-boys spilled into the room, dragging in lumps of clanging metal and panting for breath.

"What time is it?" said Luka, facing out to the garden as he heaved the exhaust pipe over the threshold.

Hazel skipped onto the worktop and pressed his nose to the kitchen clock. "Five to eight."

"You know you can see the clock from here?" said Max.

"What?" said Luka, his jacket half off. "The Domestic Warden will be here in five minutes!"

"Ah, well. I was rounding down," said Hazel. "Look."

Luka turned to the clock. "Great. We've got *two* minutes."

"At least we're back in time," said Max.

The doorbell rang.

"Oh, God! Right, Hazel," Luka stage-whispered, "you need to hide, and you need to stash this stuff somewhere!"

"Right, right—where though?" Hazel turned about in a circle.

"What about leaving it outside?" said Jem, still speaking from behind his leather mask. "If the Warden is here to check the home, and you're not to have left the building—"

"Yes!" hissed Luka. "Back outside, as quick as you can. Jem—you need to stay hidden."

Jem sighed and rolled his eyes. "Would it be so bad to be seen?"

"Well, yeah. Just finding you here would probably be enough to get us arrested. And they'd probably, like, do experiments on you."

"*Painful* experiments," added Max.

"They could try," muttered Jem, but he clambered back into Luka's sleeve and held on.

Luka rubbed his face with the dishcloth.

"How do I look?" he asked Max, raising his voice over the scrape of metal on linoleum as Hazel dragged their haul outside.

"Like you've had a fight in a scrapyard."

"Great," said Luka. He licked his thumb and wiped away a smear on Max's cheek. "Sorry," he said. "It was just right there."

The doorbell rang again as they approached the door, and they saw the Domestic Warden through the glass, huge and dark in the dim porch light.

"Ready?" whispered Luka.

"No," Max whispered back, smoothing his sweater.

"Good evening, Officer," said Luka, opening the

door. He palmed his coin and pressed it into his skin. "Lovely night. Isn't it a lovely night? Outside, I mean, I think it is—obviously we've not been out, so I'm just basing it on what I can see out the window. Don't you think so, Max?"

"That's enough, son," said the Warden. He was a hard-faced man, with a long chin, narrow eyes, and an orange-peel nose. Hugo backed up, huffing, as the officer stepped through the door, stinking of cigarettes and sweat and carrying a gray tablet. His baton swung from his belt, and his uniform seemed to exude an atmosphere all of its own, as though the heavy, fireproof fabric reeked of invisible smoke. Luka felt him filling the house, felt the wrongness of his presence like a stone in his shoe.

But he also felt Max alongside him, an ally against the invader. He moved closer to the big evacuee so that their elbows touched.

"You know the curfew starts at nightfall, son," said the Warden, looking down at them, "and that includes any private garden that may or may not be attached to your property?"

"Yessir."

"You said you've not been outside, is that correct?"

"Yessir."

The Warden thrust out his baton and raised Luka's arm.

"But you feel it necessary to wear an outdoor coat?" Luka took a deep breath. Jem, his head squashed by the baton, warily shifted his grip.

"Saving the power, sir," said Max. "For the War Effort."

The Warden shifted his attention to Max. It was like watching a steam train swivel. "You are?"

"Max Fleming, sir. Resettled for bombing."

The Warden tapped at his tablet and gave a phlegmatic cough. "Northern boy?"

"Yes."

"Parents?"

Luka glanced up.

"Dead," said Max, his face unmoving.

The Warden opened a new screen. "How?"

Max took a deep breath. Luka felt him tremble. "Air strike. Sir."

"Nothing about that here. Need to add that to your file. Didn't you tell them about this when you got to the City?"

"It's not his fault if—"

The Warden silenced Luka with a raised hand.

"I did tell them," said Max, swallowing hard.

"So, if you're saving power for maximum War Effort, Max, how come he's"—the Warden rapped his knuckle against Luka's forehead—"the only one wearing a coat?"

Luka stared at the Warden's gigantic hand.

"He is a delicate little boy," said Max confidently.

The Warden raised an eyebrow at Luka. "Is that true, son?"

Luka's ears shot back as he grimaced.

"Yes," he said. "I'm a delicate little boy."

The Warden stood back and appraised the two of them. "Makes sense," he said. He typed something into his tablet.

Jem began to tremble, as though suppressing laughter. Luka slapped his sleeve.

"Ow!" he said.

The Warden looked up and raised his eyebrows.

"Pins and needles," said Luka quickly, shaking his wrist.

"First night alone," said the Warden, scanning the hallway. "Mother's an engineer, gone for . . ." He checked his tablet. "One week?"

"Yessir."

"Let's start in the kitchen, shall we?"

"You're checking the house?" said Luka, slamming the front door and skipping to overtake the Warden. "The whole house?"

The Warden took off his helmet and smoothed his greasy hair under his palm.

"It is mandatory for the unaccompanied children of active service personnel to receive a thorough home inspection at the beginning of their solo stay," he parroted from the textbook in his head. "Should the inspection prove . . . *unsatisfactory* . . . for any reason, the child or children in that household should be taken into the City's care within a designated custodial residence. So, yes. I'll check the whole house." He pressed chewing tobacco under his top lip and gave them an oily smile. "Is that a problem?"

"Not at all," said Luka. "Starting in the kitchen, you said? The *kitchen*?"

The Warden swished his thick tobacco spit, narrowed his eyes, and pushed the kitchen door open.

Seeing it through the Warden's eyes, Luka realized just how messy it was: there were plates of discarded crusts, pots of knife-stuck butter and jam, a little forest of half-full mugs, and a stack of sticky glasses.

"Not a great start, boys," said the Warden. He tapped at his screen. "You feeding yourselves adequately, and making full use of the rations?"

"Um . . . yeah," said Luka. "Mostly . . . hot drinks for warmth. And carbohydrates. For energy."

The Warden blinked slowly at him. "Do you mean tea and toast, son?"

"Yessir."

"With a wide range of toppings," said Max, pointing to the jars.

"Uh-huh," said the Warden. "You know that failure to feed yourselves properly, accounting for all the main food groups, is sufficient cause for concern that you could both be taken into custody immediately, yes?"

Luka, remembering the spaniel in the scrapyard, had a flash of inspiration.

"I had a sausage this morning," he said.

"Congratulations," said the Warden, checking his tablet. "Your sister has been evacuated to the Islands, is that correct?"

"Yessir."

"So, it's just the two of you living here?"

"Yessir."

"Then why are there three plates on that table?" The Warden waited, his enormous face lit from below by the tablet's screen, hand poised over the keyboard.

"We had a visitor this morning," said Luka, at the exact moment that Max said, "That's his mum's breakfast."

The Warden's eyebrows moved upward.

"She works so much," said Luka, biting his lip as Jem squeezed his forearm. "It was like having a visitor in the house."

"And your mother, the visitor to her own home— she eats standing on the furniture, does she?"

Luka glanced at the table, which was covered in the muddy traces of Hazel's feet.

"Yes," said Luka, wondering, as the lie unspooled before him like a roll of film, why he didn't say something—*anything*—else. "Those are her footprints."

"And she wears a men's shoe, does she?" said the Warden, measuring the tread against his pencil.

"For balance," said Max.

"Yes," said Luka, glancing at him. "She's quite a character, my mum."

"She falls over a lot?" said the Warden, typing.

"Not," said Luka, speaking carefully, as though stepping across a lightly frozen pond, "since she got the shoes."

The Warden shifted his wad of tobacco to the other cheek.

"So, what you're telling me is that your mother—a five-foot-tall, high-ranking engineer aged forty-three—wears a size ten men's boot and eats breakfast standing on the table to make sure she doesn't fall over?"

Luka turned to Max, who nodded.

"That's what we're telling you," said Luka.

"This smells funny to me, boys," said the Warden. "And I don't like funny."

"We appreciate that, sir," said Max.

"Can we have a look upstairs?"

"Of course. Let's just go back into the *hallway* right now!"

The Warden slapped a hand on Luka's chest. "You always announce your passage through the home in this manner, son?"

"Of course," said Luka, appearing and vanishing

his coin across a sweating palm. "Doesn't everyone?"

The Warden kicked open the kitchen door and went first into the hall. Hugo shot between his legs, and the Warden stumbled.

"Damn dog!" he shouted, balancing against the wall.

Luka glanced over the man's head and saw Hazel, wedged into the corner of the far hallway wall and ceiling like a scruffy, grinning Spider-Man.

Hi, Rake, he mouthed.

Luka flashed him a look. "Let's check out the upstairs then, shall we?" he said brightly, leading the way.

Max followed Luka's gaze. "Yes," he said. "Now is definitely the time to go upstairs."

The Warden's brow furrowed. He took a step forward and stumbled over something in his path. "What was that?"

Luka gasped. Jem's bird-skull mask was now sitting under the radiator, its little eyeholes staring right at the Warden. "Let me see!" he said quickly, leaping to the ground. He palmed the helmet, pushing it into the secret pocket of his left sleeve. "Well, what do you know? I don't see anything here."

"Where'd it go?" said the Warden.

"It must have been just a bit of fluff," said Luka, flexing his empty hands. "You saw the fluff, right, Max?"

Max nodded. "Couldn't believe how fluffy this house was when I arrived. There's fluff everywhere."

The Warden looked between them, then stepped back, nudging a framed photo of Luka's family, which swung on its hook. "Let's check the bedrooms."

"Right this way," said Luka.

They tramped up the stairs, Luka hauling his weak leg with a hand on his jeans.

"Steady . . ." whispered Jem.

Luka checked Hazel's hiding spot. But he was nowhere in sight.

"Which is the evacuee's accommodation?" asked the Warden, panting rancidly over them with the exertion of the steps.

"This one," said Luka, pushing the door. "This is my sis—it's Max's room." Out of the corner of his eye, he saw Max smile.

The Warden peered inside.

"Very tidy," he muttered. "Not got much stuff, I expect."

"No," said Max. "It was all destroyed."

"And your own accommodation?" said the Warden, turning back to Luka.

"Um, it's—" Luka began, remembering, with a sinking feeling, Hazel's unzipped bags of hi-tech, top-secret, stolen military equipment.

He looked at Max, who gave him a panicked shrug.

"It's a bit untidy just now—"

"It's not scout camp, son. I just need to check the dwelling. Your room, please."

Luka shuffled reluctantly across the hall. "O—kay, here we—" He froze in the doorway. Every surface in his bedroom, every shelf, was immaculate. "—are!"

The Warden prowled into the room and sniffed.

"Smells like plants in here. That your hammock, son?"

"What? Oh, yes, I—" Luka's voice trailed away as he saw the hammock's deep, slow swing—and realized that Hazel was *in* his hammock.

"Used to have one of these when I were a lad," said the Warden, crossing the room with slow, deliberate steps. "Comfy things; they are best kept outside though—"

The lightbulb exploded over his head, showering his helmet with hot glass and plunging the room into instant darkness.

Luka felt a rush of wind as Hazel flew past him. Max laughed.

"What? What did you do?" cried the Warden, turning the hammock upside down. "Someone was—"

"Are you all right, sir?" said Luka. "I'll replace that bulb, we have plenty of spares. Or we'll save power and stick with candles. Max?"

"Candles," said Max. "War Effort, innit?"

Luka clapped his hands together and started to back out into the hallway. "Candles it is! That must have given you a real fright! I know I could use a cup of tea. Max?"

"Tea would calm *me* down," Max agreed.

"But . . . but . . . there was a . . ." said the Warden, his ears reddening. "There's something going on here. I know there is." He looked at them both, then stormed from the room.

"Are you sure you don't want tea?" Luka called after him, hopping down the stairs as quickly as he could.

"I'll be back tomorrow!" the Warden shouted as he slammed the door. "And I'll be keeping my eye on you!" The clash of the door echoed through the house.

Hazel popped his head over the banister and grinned. Jem poked his head from Luka's sleeve and waggled a blowgun between his fingers.

"Shot that bulb out first time," he said. "I'll eat what's left of the filament, if you don't mind. And you'd better get me a nice, thick roof tile *this second*—or I'll bite off your elbows."

30

The scrap had been stowed in the kitchen cupboard, and the plates and mugs piled tidily in the sink.

"You're doing a decent job there," said Jem, biting into his third roof tile of the night. He hopped onto a bag of rice, which folded around him like a beanbag. A single candle behind him threw a flickering glow over the dark walls.

"Thanks," said Luka. "I thought you *liked* doing chores?"

"We like *helping*, biggun. And I think constantly bailing you out against your many enemies is plenty on that score, don't you?"

"He's right, Rake. Besides, the place looks good."

Luka ran his eye over the kitchen. "It looks better. But you're standing on the cheese."

"Oh," said Hazel, dropping to the floor, plasticky cheese stuck to his heel. "It's as good as it's going to get anyway. Now, let's hit the hay—I'm beat."

"Bed?" said Luka. "Now?"

"Well, yeah. It's bedtime."

"But—" Luka lifted his arm, letting the chain swing between him and Jem. "How am I meant to sleep with a vengeful faerie handcuffed to my arm?"

Jem took another bite of slate.

Hazel shrugged. "Fitfully?"

"Stay positive," said Max.

"Are you out of your mind? We need to take these off, I can't sleep like—"

"Ah, come on," said Jem, stuffing tobacco in his pipe as Luka followed the others upstairs. "What's the worst that could happen?"

"You were talking about eating my eyeballs earlier. Now I'm expected to be relaxed about you sleeping next to my face?"

"I'm full now," said Jem, burping out flecks of slate. "Your biggest concern is my snoring." He reached over and scratched the top of Hugo's head. The big dog's foot thumped on the kitchen tiles. "This animal is growing on me, I must say."

Hazel leaped into his hammock and swung happily back and forth. "Ah, I *can* see my tower from here. I wonder if there's a Warden hiding in it, waiting for me to come back."

Luka scanned the empty floor. "What did you do with all your stuff?"

"It's under your bed. Along with a lot of rubbish, I might add. You really need to wash some of those mugs, Rake. Disgusting."

He ran his hand over his head, then divided a chunk of hair into sections before splitting it into two parts.

"What are you doing?" said Luka.

Hazel, twisting the strands through his fingers, rolled his eyes.

"You don't think these twists happen by themselves, do you?" He produced a little bottle and squeezed three drops onto his palm. "You might be content to walk around under an unruly mop," he added, working the oil over his scalp, "but I have *standards*."

"I'm going to brush my teeth," said Luka, leaving Hazel swinging happily behind him. He looked at Jem. "With my other hand, I guess."

Jem balanced on his shoulder, and together they peered into the bathroom mirror. "How do humans survive with such delicate teeth?"

"I don't know. We don't eat roof tiles, I guess. What are yours made of? Granite?" said Luka, squeezing out his ration of toothpaste.

"All the better for biting your knuckles off."

"You don't need to—" Luka sighed, foam on his lips. "You can let some of those chances pass." He spat and turned out the light. Then, before he went into his room, he knocked lightly on Elena's bedroom door and pushed it open.

Max was changing into a baggy T-shirt. High on his bare shoulder blade, in the middle of a whirlpool of skin, was a deep, purple scar.

"Sorry," said Luka, "I just—"

"It's okay," said Max, dropping the T-shirt over his

head and holding out the logo on the front. "This was my old man's."

Luka nodded.

"I'm sorry about . . . I didn't realize about your mum and dad."

Max nodded. "I'm sorry about your dad."

Jem cleared his throat. "That's a lovely scar. Where'd you get it?"

Max climbed into bed and blew out his candle. "None of your business, little bro," he said.

"Ah, come on," said the faerie, lifting his shirt to reveal a sculpted torso. "We can compare! This is one of my favorites: one of the Elder Guard rats turned against us, and—"

"Good *night*, little man," said Max, exhaustion in his voice.

Luka slipped into his own bed, Hugo at his feet and Jem at his shoulder. The faerie ground his teeth and sniffed irritably.

"I was just trying to be friendly. Faeries love scars; they show you've lived." He tossed his tiny boots onto the floor.

The two of them lay awhile, Luka listening to the thrum of the faerie's rapid heart through the mattress.

"You know, Rake," said Hazel, his voice softening with fatigue. "I meant it when I said I wasn't spying on you guys, not really. It's just . . . you were this perfect family, and I was on my own out there. I just . . . I wanted to be part of what you had. And now that I am here, I'll help keep it safe. We can protect the house together. Our weird little family."

Luka felt his cheeks flush in the dark. "All right."

"G'night," said Hazel.

Luka checked his curfew-blank phone and blinked at the ceiling, tracing the cracks in the paint as he always did. He cast his mind back to how it had been before the War, whispering conversations with Elena across the hallway though their open doors, unburdened and carefree, ignorant to the world that lived on the other side of the shadows in his garden.

He thought about sprinting with Jem to the top of the crane, and what it had felt like to leap out a hundred feet in the air before they slid down the cable. His blood fizzed with the memory.

Scars show you've lived, he thought.

"Thank you for helping me today," he whispered. "I couldn't have done any of that without you."

"You definitely could not," said Jem. "But you did well. You're either very brave or very stubborn. You can sleep now." He chuckled, weapons chiming as he turned onto his side. "You're quite safe."

"Really?"

"Absolutely. There's no honor in killing a sleeping enemy."

"That's a real comfort."

Hazel was already snoring gently in his hammock, and presently Jem dropped into a rasping breath. Luka, mind bright and awake, swiped open the photo he'd taken of Hazel in front of his tower, desperate and screaming, seconds before Luka had tripped and drawn over the Warden.

He dragged it to the dustbin, feeling a queasy weight settle in his stomach, and read through his old chats with Elena.

He thought about her, surrounded by painful iron, only a day from slipping permanently into the world of the faeries.

"It's not going to happen, Ellie," he said aloud. "I'll stop them, even if it kills me."

Slowly, gradually, exhaustion smothered him in its heavy cloak. He closed his eyes, and while the house lay at peace, Luka's dreaming mind roiled with roof tiles, Wardens, and shining teeth; with frosted glasses, rusting masks, and voices that whispered while coins fell from his palms, and his sister lay still under an iron sky.

31

Jem was sitting on Luka's chest, sharpening his father's sword. "Morning," he said with a wink. "Lovely bright winter's day it is."

Luka let his head fall back onto the pillow. The faerie's weight was incredible, as though his tiny frame was filled with lead.

"You couldn't give me a couple of seconds to feel normal?" he said. "You know, with no eldritch creatures threatening to kill me the second I wake up, that sort of thing."

Jem shrugged and sheathed his sword. "No sense hiding from the inevitable. Up you get," he said, leaping from the bed and dragging Luka face-first onto the floor.

"Ooft! Give me a minute, will you?"

"Nope," said Jem, striding into the hall, Luka flapping behind him like a fish out of water as Hugo barked and skipped around.

"I hope the other two have prepared me some good slate for breakfast. I've been eating rabbit for days. My ears are getting longer just thinking about it."

He hopped onto the banister.

"Wait," said Luka. "Jem—"

Jem kicked off just as Luka jumped on behind him, and together they slid down the stairs.

"You can't *do* that," shouted Luka as they slid off the end. "I could have broken my neck!"

"But you didn't, did you?" said Jem, pushing the kitchen door.

Max was sitting at the table, and Hazel—welder's mask fixed to his head—was cross-legged on the worktop. Both were chewing bread and butter, and a pot was bubbling on the stove, a pair of spindly black legs poking from under its lid.

Luka sniffed. The air smelled steamy and damp. "What's in the pot?" he said warily.

Hazel grinned, then sprinkled some seasoning from his pockets into the bubbling liquid.

"Found a big magpie when I was up on the roof," he said. "Lucky, eh?"

Luka sniffed again. "*So* lucky."

Jem smacked his lips.

"That smells good," he said. "Perhaps I'll spread its kidneys on my breakfast slate."

Luka covered his mouth.

"Don't worry, Rake—it won't be ready for hours yet."

"That's not what was worrying me, *Brains*."

Jem ran up Luka's leg and vaulted onto the table. "Slate, please."

Hazel slid a plate toward the faerie. Luka *thunked* a piece of bread into the toaster.

"I miss real peanut butter," he said, opening a jar and spooning out the thin, gray paste inside.

Max added water to a capsule of powdered avocado, squinting as he stirred.

"How long have you guys been up?" Luka asked.

"Long enough," said Hazel. "I welded that bit of fence we cut out onto the window in the downstairs toilet, then I managed to fix a fender to the windowsill on Max's room—"

"Which is what woke me up," said Max, peering through half-shut eyes.

"And we've got the rest of today to get more welding done. Then, as soon as it's dark I'll—"

"You know the Reckoning is *tomorrow*, right?" Luka interrupted.

"Uh, yeah," said Hazel. "Like I said, we'll finish welding what we have today, then we'll go get more stuff."

"This is going to be a seriously long day," said Luka, spreading his faux-nut butter. "I can't believe—"

A thunderclap sounded over the house, and the high-pitched screech of machinery filled the air.

"It's a raid!" shouted Max.

Hazel leaped at the window, peering outside. "Can't be!" he said. "No siren!"

"Hazel!" yelled Luka. "Get down!"

"*Look!*" shouted Hazel, pointing.

A huge gray aircraft was coasting toward the ground, white smoke belching from its guts, flames sputtering from its engines. They watched the pilot eject, the white arc of a parachute bright in the morning sun.

"What was *that*?" said Luka, joining Hazel at the window.

"I've no idea! There weren't even any insignia on that plane. That means it's"—Hazel was almost drooling—"*top secret*. And it's crashed. Near Wildwood Park!"

"Oh my God," said Luka. "That's serious."

"Seriously good news!" said Hazel. "This is brilliant!"

"How, Hazel? How is this brilliant? They're probably going to shut the network down *again* for this." Luka dashed around the kitchen. "Where's my phone?"

"Think about it," said Hazel, his eyes wide. "All that wreckage—just lying there."

"A crashed plane?" said Max. "Are we going for another serious crime?"

Hazel waved his hands above his head. "They can only hold so many crimes against you. We're probably maxed out after last night."

Max shook his head. "I'm really sure that's not true."

"*Anyway*," said Hazel, waving his hands, "let's get on the scanner and find out where it is!"

"Won't it be on the news?" said Luka, clicking on the TV.

A helicopter was already covering the scene, showing a furrow of scorched parkland ending in a pile of smoking metal.

Hazel grabbed the remote. "They're not going to tell you *where* it is on the *TV*—that's classified information. To normal people, that is. Not to the Wild Huntsboys."

A banner was scrolling along the bottom of the screen.

WI-FI AND DATA NETWORKS SHUT DOWN——MATTER OF CITY SECURITY, SAYS GOVT——NO TIMELINE RELEASED FOR REINSTATEMENT——

Luka found his phone and swiped it open.

> DIGITAL CURFEW – IMMEDIATE – NO TIMELINE RELEASED FOR REINSTATEMENT –

There were no bars, no data, no Wi-Fi.

No Elena.

"Come *on*!" he said. "This is unbelievable. Can't you do something, Hazel? I just want to know she's okay."

"Sorry, Rake—I can hide what I'm doing online,

but I still need the network to do it. But listen, she'll be fine until tomorrow night, right, Jem?"

"Yes," said Jem quietly. "Though she'll be in great pain. And very afraid."

Luka closed his eyes. "We need to fix this. *I* need to fix this."

"So, let's find that plane," said Hazel, pushing his headphones into his ears and twiddling the dials on his watch. Tiny hissing voices reached Luka's ears, shouting among the static that hissed from the little speaker.

Hazel opened his eyes. "The *marshes*," he said. "Of course, that's why the fire was out already—it landed in the water!"

"We're going there now?" said Jem, hopping forward, sword in hand.

The Wild Huntsboys looked at him.

"You seem very keen," said Luka.

Jem cleared his throat and flashed his dark teeth. "It is a question of honor. You put yourself at risk to retrieve my sword, and your . . . your sister's pain wounds you more deeply than your own. I am wounded myself to see it, knowing my part in its creation."

Luka followed the handcuffs' chain with his eyes, and felt another surge of power flow through him. His heart gave a little thump.

"What are you saying?" said Max, taking a step forward.

Jem rolled his eyes, then gave a dramatic swish of his sword and grinned.

"I'm saying that I wish to help you Wild Hunts-boys. I have always admired the human capacity for courage, and for love. And I see it in you."

"Love?" said Hazel. "Oh, yeah. We love each other, right, boys?"

The three of them laughed nervously.

"You can joke," said Jem, finishing his slate. "But these eyes of mine can see what's in front of them. I'll help you."

"Can we trust him?" said Max.

Jem spread his arms. "Am I burning?"

"He isn't, you know," said Hazel. "I reckon we can trust him."

Jem nodded. "You can. And even if you think I'm somehow lying, what have you got to lose? Apart from everything." He extended his hand.

"That's one way to put it," said Luka, looking at the faerie's tiny, hard fingers. They shook, and Hugo barked in agreement.

"Great!" said Hazel. "Now we're five! Get the bag, Muscles, and let's find that plane before anyone else does."

"Wait," said Max, "we're not waiting until it gets dark?"

"Nope," said Luka, strength moving through his veins as Jem climbed onto his shoulder. "We need as much iron as we can find, as quickly as we can get it. Besides, there's nothing there we can't handle, right?"

Max frowned. "Apart from God knows how many Wardens *and* probably the Lost Boys with their masks and baseball bats. In bright daylight."

"You heard the man," said Hazel, clapping his hands and grinning. "Nothing we can't handle—we're the Wild Huntsboys!"

32

Golden coins of sunlight dappled the visualizer's screen. Luka shaded it, Jem peering down from his shoulder. "I can't see anything," he said, rubbing his hands together and stamping his feet.

"That's good," said Hazel.

"No—I can't see *anything*. It's too bright."

Hazel was up a tree, almost hidden in the branches. He scanned the crash site with steady sweeps of the isolator, looking for the telltale squares of the Wardens' helmets.

"Just keep looking, Rakey," he said. "And put that phone away."

Luka sighed. "There's no network, you know. I just wanted to see if—"

"You think they can't track you anyway? Make sure it's switched off, you're like a bloody homing beacon."

"I still think we should have waited till it was dark," said Max. "It's hard to pretend you're not up to something when you're wearing a homemade ski mask."

Hugo whined and pawed the ground. He was wearing a saddlebag made from an old pillowcase.

"You look cool," said Luka. "Don't worry. You seem very at home with all this," he added, turning to Max.

"What do you mean?"

"All this . . . mission control stuff. Planning missions and tracking people."

Max shrugged. "It's no big deal."

"It is," said Luka. "It might not be to Brains, with his stolen equipment, or to Jem with his charmed birds and swords. Where *did* you get that scar?"

Max turned away.

"Nowhere," he said. "It's nothing. I told you, don't—"

"It's not—"

Jem squeezed Luka's ear.

"Best left," he whispered. "A man deserves to keep his secrets."

"A what?" said Luka.

"We've got a visitor," said Hazel, waving for quiet.

The others scrambled to their feet and peered out over the marsh. The fallen plane lay a hundred yards away in a tangle of shredded black metal.

"I don't see anyone," said Luka. He held his breath and waited for the fog to dissipate.

"There," said Hazel, pointing to the right of the plane.

"Is it the Wardens?"

Hazel clicked the isolator's dial and waited. "Nope," he said. With the thin sunlight behind him, his head was merely an outline against the glow. "It's *him*."

Luka watched the Junkyard Knight step onto the

plane's wing, a canvas sack strapped to his back, a baseball bat in his ungloved hands. "Great," he said. "Where are the Wardens when you need them?"

Hazel leaped down and scurried over to his tech bag. "Probably waiting for looters so they can arrest them. We need to get over there."

"This was a mistake, wasn't it?" said Luka.

Hazel looked up and grinned. There were coffee smears on his teeth. "Nah," he said. "It'll be fine. Right, Jem?"

Jem nodded. "I have good feelings," he said. "Mind you, I like fighting."

"Oh, God," said Luka. "What if—"

"There are no *ifs*, Rake. There's only what happens and what doesn't. And right now, we're getting what we need." He put his hand in the middle of their circle, into the cloud of their shared breath. Max placed his on top.

Luka settled his thumping heart, then thumped down his own hand and gripped their knuckles.

"I can't reach," said Jem. "But I'm in."

Hugo nosed their gathered hands.

"Ready, Huntsboys?" said Hazel, turning to the open marshland.

"Yes," said Luka, gripping his coin.

They burst from the cover of the tree, the wind whipping their faces as the sky opened overhead.

Already the site was crawling with Lost Boys, tearing and stabbing at the plane like bugs on a carcass. The Junkyard Knight looked up, then raised his bat. The Lost Boys turned.

"And there he is—Lucky Luka!" he shouted, jumping onto the ground and holding his bat in the air. He began to chant, a deep ululation that was picked up by the others in a communal howl.

"You're going to lose!" Luka shouted, his hand locked on Hugo's straining collar. "You know that, don't you?"

The Knight spread his arms and smiled. "We are already Lost," he said. "This wreckage is ours, and no one can stop us."

He lowered his bat and the Lost Boys charged.

At the same moment, dozens of Wardens rose from the ground, all blank faces with shrill whistles and hands grabbing at the passing masks.

"It begins!" roared the Junkyard Knight, laughing hysterically as he swung his bat at a Warden's helmet.

"He's crackers," said Max.

"Run!" shouted Luka.

A vanguard of Lost Boys charged the Huntsboys, scattering them across the field, only to be scattered themselves by Hugo's snapping jaws.

"You ready?" Luka shouted.

"Always," said Jem, gripping tight.

Luka's arm spun to the right, knocking a Lost Boy on his backside, then pirouetted behind him to trip another. The two lay in a heap, their bats twisted beneath them.

"I'm getting used to this," said Luka.

"Battle-lust!" shouted Jem. "Oh, how it warms the blood!"

With Hugo loping alongside, Luka dodged the swiping arms of a bearded Warden and headed straight for the Junkyard Knight.

He was in the middle of a circle of Wardens, keeping them at bay with wild swings as he shouted and swore.

Luka barreled through the crowd, allowing Jem to lead, feeling the intoxicating power flowing through him as he flew through the air and hit the Knight's waist with his shoulder.

They rolled down the hill, grabbing at each other, and landed, soaking, in the freezing marsh.

"Lucky Luka!" roared the Knight, getting to his feet and aiming a kick at Luka's belly. "You really don't know when you're beaten, do you?"

Jem pulled Luka to the side, then heaved him upright and swung his fist against the rusted mask.

The Junkyard Knight flew backward, sliding over the mud.

"You've lost now, numbnuts!" he shouted.

"Good line," said Jem. "Now, onward!"

Wardens were piling over the marsh as Luka ran back toward the plane. He saw Max and Hugo in the midst of a crowd; Max was using one of the Lost Boys as a shield to keep the others at bay.

"Where's Brains?" he shouted, sliding between the knees of another grabbing Warden.

All over the marsh, there were Lost Boys being led away in handcuffs, their masks torn away to reveal soft-faced, sobbing children.

"In the aircraft," said Jem after a moment.

"What? What's he doing in—"

The plane's tailfin tore with a deafening shriek, and Hazel's face appeared in the hole. "All right, Rake?" he said, grinning. "Figure this'll do nicely, what you reckon?"

"Yes!" shouted Luka. "Just grab it and let's go! We can't—"

He was interrupted by sirens and the screech of brakes and looked up to see a van behind the trees, its door spilling more Wardens—and the Trenchcoat, who stared out over the battlefield through his frosted spectacles. He was joined by a woman in an identical coat and glasses. Then another. And another. Acting as one, the Trenchcoats shone a laser pointer on Hazel's forehead, then turned to Luka and Max and did the same.

"Oh, no no no," said Hazel, pulling at the tailfin and scrambling to the ground. "This is bad, this is very bad, we need to get out of here!"

All around, the Wardens were dropping the Lost

Boys and turning to the Huntsboys, their earpieces
blinking with a new, red light.

"They've marked us!" shouted Luka.

"No more battle?" said Jem.

"No! We need to go, they're *really* after us now!"
He took the other end of the tailfin and ran with Hazel
toward the trees, watching the tide of Wardens turn to
follow.

"Muscles!" called Hazel, and Max pushed his assailants backward, falling into step with Hugo at his
heels.

"We'll be okay once we get to the trees," panted Hazel, his feet slopping in and out of the soggy ground.
"Just get to the trees!"

Luka dared a glance over his shoulder.

The Wardens had formed a solid mass and were giving chase with stern expressions, their boots pounding
the soggy ground. Behind them, the Trenchcoat glowered, his feet sunk in the marshy ground, his hand in
the vacant space in the plane's tail.

"Get them!" he screamed, his voice unnervingly
shrill in the panicked silence of the chase.

The Wardens redoubled their efforts.

But their feet were slowing as they trudged through
the mud.

"We're going to make it!" shouted Luka. "Look!"

One Warden fell face-first, tripping another and
dropping more to their knees. The rest plowed on,

driving their boots farther into the marsh—one lifted her leg high enough to reveal a startling white sock before falling beside her comrades.

"Nearly there!" shouted Luka. He pushed with every ounce of strength he had, his weak leg screaming in protest, his free hand gripping Hugo's collar—then Max appeared behind him, pushing him forward; Hazel tugged on the tailfin; and Jem leaped from his sleeve, jolting them all toward the shade of the trees and leaving a roiling mass of stricken Wardens in the marsh, their frustrated shouts bouncing from the clouds as the Huntsboys vanished into the forest.

33

"You feeling all right?" said Luka. "Even with carrying this iron?"

Jem, his jaw tight, nodded. The sun lanced in through Luka's bedroom window, throwing the bloodied handprint across the floor in a long, thin shadow.

"So long as I'm in my suit, I'll be fine," the faerie said, leaning his forehead against the glass.

Hazel flipped up his welder's mask. "We ready then?"

Max hefted the tailfin onto his shoulder. "Where will this go?"

"I reckon I can split it into three parts," said Hazel, running his hand along the smooth surface and spinning his welding rod. "That way I'll get Rake's window finished *and* get started on his sister's room. This thing alone is nearly half what we need—we'll definitely get it done at this rate!"

Ellie, thought Luka. *We might actually do this.*

"What do those pictures mean?" he said.

"No idea." Max angled the metal to catch the sunlight.

"They're not *pictures*," said Hazel, rolling his eyes. "They're the insignia. I thought there weren't any at first, but they're just tiny. That's the flying corps, that's the pilot's rank, and the mission design series is . . ." He took the tailfin from Max and turned it round, running his hands along the flaps. "Well, this is odd."

"What is?" said Luka.

"There isn't one."

Luka shared a look with Max. "One what? Hazel, remember who you're talking to."

Hazel waved a dismissive hand. "A mission design series. Every aircraft has one, like . . . B-52 or F-15 or whatever. But if this plane didn't even *have* one, then . . ." He sat back on his haunches, his eyes glowing.

"Then what?" said Max.

"Then I was right—it *is* top secret!" said Hazel. "This must be a totally new type of plane, and it's not even been officially stamped by the flying corps. I have to get back to that crash site, if we can—"

"Hazel!" said Luka. "We can't go back *there*! The Trenchcoat marked you with a laser pointer. He knows who you are and he knows we've got this! We've stolen his secret plane—he'll be looking for us right now."

Hazel leaped to his feet and heaved the big window open. The afternoon sun was bright on the flat roof, and it burned hot and white in their eyes.

"Grab that band saw, would you, Rake?" he said, taking the tailfin's tip from Max and planting his feet on the windowsill.

Luka turned to the massed piles of Hazel's equipment. "We really need to clear this stuff away before the Domestic comes back tonight," he said, picking up the first thing that looked vaguely saw-like. Hazel laughed.

"Try again, Rakey. No. No. No. The blue one. That's teal. *Blue*. That's it!"

"I'd call this turquoise," Luka muttered.

"I'd agree," said Jem.

Luka handed Hazel the band saw and watched as he began to slice the tailfin into thin strips.

Narrowing his eyes to dim the sparks, Luka moved toward the window, and the shadow of the bloody handprint flashed across his belly. He paused.

"What is it?" said Jem.

"Just, thank you. I still can't believe you're helping us."

Jem tilted his head. "You're welcome," he said.

The handcuffs' chain shifted between them, and Luka fancied he could feel the faerie's heartbeat through the metal.

"Let's go, Huntsboys," called Hazel. "We're nearly there! Then, tonight, on to the train station!"

"Maybe we can do this." Max laughed, shaking his head.

Luka pulled on his weak leg and hauled himself onto the roof, next to the others and the torn strips of metal. Hugo planted his feet on the windowsill and yelped, his tail wagging frantically.

"Get down!" said Luka, pushing the dog's cold nose. "We'll be back in a minute, just—"

"That's not why he's barking," said Jem, his voice hard.

"What? Why else would—" Luka turned to see Hazel and Max frozen in mid-lurch, the tailfin stretched out between them. A crow was watching them from the center of the roof's bright square, its black eyes unblinking and calm. But it wasn't the bird that had stopped the Huntsboys in their tracks. It was the faerie mounted on its back.

"Esme," said Jem. "I knew you'd come."

34

Elena knew her body was in the bed, just as she knew there were clouds in the sky and currents in the sea, but her mind floated ever farther from it as the iron seeped ever deeper into her body.

She felt the steel of the abattoir clanging like cymbals in her ears, as though its white heat was being held against her skin, and the shrill wail of the data mast on the hill needled steadily toward her.

She felt it in the earth now—the seams of ancient ore that ran through the island's soil in tremulous waves; the pull of the earth's magnetic poles splitting her apart cell by cell. Her hair crackled with invisible sparks, and her skin had begun to thin, her veins bright and blue in her wrists.

She dreamed without sleeping of the faeries she had invited into her home, of the instinctive connection she'd felt to them—of the secret rituals she'd seen them perform, and the worry she'd felt when she was told she'd be leaving her home and traveling to the Islands.

She dreamed also of the promise Luka had made her, and the heartache she nursed at his instant betrayal.

But she felt something else, another force beating through the swirling ether of her mind: his love for her, bright and hot as a flame, and his desire to set things right. To make her well and break the curse.

"Luka," she whispered, her mouth dry. "Keep trying. You can do it, I know you can—keep trying!"

She clung to the warmth of her brother's love like a life raft as the world's iron beat through her veins.

35

Luka studied the new faerie. Esme was a little taller than Jem, but had the same shock of red hair and alabaster skin. Like Jem, her eyes were black, and her lips the deep red of old blood. When she spoke, her voice was dry and hard.

"Jem. How are the humans treating you?"

"Well," said Jem, unmoving.

Luka stared at him. He'd never heard the faerie sound so flat, so empty of character. Even when they'd first been chained together, his anger had been so vivid and bright.

Esme hopped onto the roof, and Hazel and Max stepped back. "I come with a message," she said, tapping the heel of her boot against the chimney pot.

"Is that all?" said Hazel, sagging with relief. "Listen, we're getting on fine. I get him all the roof tiles he can eat. Mostly from next door, to be fair, but—"

Esme raised her hand. "We have been watching, as you knew we would."

Jem nodded.

"You knew?" said Luka. "I thought *you* were the watcher? Why didn't you tell us?"

"Thank you, mistress," said Jem, his eyes fixed straight ahead.

Esme looked around at the Huntsboys, her face curling in distaste. "We have noted your capture, and the efforts of these . . . boys . . . to protect themselves from the Reckoning. For both these reasons the council has issued a decree: the Reckoning on this marked house will be at the stroke of midnight, tonight, and you will be freed by the severing of the insulter's hand—"

"What?" shouted Luka, striding forward and shoving past Max. "That's not fair! I get three moons! That's *your* law!"

Esme smirked and squinted up at him. "Our laws exist to protect the lore," she said. "And in taking your body parts we *do* protect it."

"But—"

"*You* spilled the offering," she said, "on the very tree that binds us to this house. Even now, this cowardly act drains the life from your poor sister—she who so faithfully kept our pact—and your attempts to—"

"Please," said Luka, dropping to his knees. Tears sprang to his eyes, and he felt his heart skip with an extra, painful beat. "You have to save her. Take me, cut off my hand, do whatever you want to me—but save Ellie, please!"

Jem pressed his hand flat against Luka's head and gripped his hair.

Esme's eyes were cold. "We cannot stop Elena's fate," she said. "The iron will find her and she will become ours. It is you who has made this happen. Not us."

Luka closed his eyes, the sun glowing hot and red through his lids as he wept. He thought of Elena far off on the Islands, lying among the wreckage of his broken promise, her energy leaking away into the world of the fairfolk. He wondered if she could still see the sun and feel its heat.

"Jem," said Esme. "You offer no comfort to your captors, I trust?"

"No," said Jem. "They are my enemy, as they are yours. They broke the pact with knowing hearts and they disrespected the lore. When the Reckoning comes, as it must, I will be ready."

Luka felt the faerie's betrayal beat like poisoned oil through his veins. He turned away from Jem.

But then he felt it—the faerie was gripping his scalp with a hand that burned like molten steel.

Luka's eyes flashed open. He smelled his burning hair and felt the heat of Jem's lie scorch his scalp. He bit his lip to smother the pain—to keep Jem's secret hidden.

"It is well," said Esme, as Jem's hand began to tremble. "I will return. There will be others. They will have blades."

She vaulted onto the crow's back and pulled it about

by the scruff of its neck. The bird flapped and rose, the shadow of its wingspan flashing over the Huntsboys.

Then she was gone, climbing into the sky over the park until she could have been just another drone hovering over the stricken City.

"You little wretch!" hissed Max, dropping the tailfin and stomping over to Jem.

"Yeah!" said Hazel. "I thought you were helping us! But as soon as she—"

"Wait!" Luka jumped to his feet and put himself between them and Jem. He held the faerie at arm's length, his body trembling under the little man's weight. "He *is* on our side—look."

He placed Jem on the roof, then tilted his head toward his friends.

Max examined Luka's scorched skin. "This must have been agony," he said after a moment.

Luka nodded, trying to ignore the pain. He looked at Jem. "Are *you* all right?"

The faerie nodded, then grimaced as he pressed his red-hot hand to the cold roof.

"I thought for a moment she would spot it, so I pressed it onto you. I'm sorry. It was the only way to prevent my eyes from revealing the deceit. The lore is a betrayal of what I have always known in my heart to be right, and I will no longer fly its flag. You seek only to protect your sister, I know *that* in my heart, and your comrades stand with you against overwhelming odds.

This is what I love about humans—your courage and your hearts. It is what the fairfolk fear about you most of all, because it is that bond that makes you strong."

He sat up and leaned against the chimney stack.

"My kind have long suspected me of what they call weakness. I am *not* weak. I will fight and I will die for the right cause. But if preservation of the lore means punishing the innocent, then that is wrong and I can no longer stand behind it."

"But I'm not innocent," said Luka, his burned skin starting to blister. "I spilled the offering. I did it."

Jem shook his head. "A mind suffering the trauma of loss is not a rational place. Your sister is gone. Your father is dead. Your mother labors far from home. I know what stormy seas a mind sails in such circumstances, and I will not be party to your punishment."

More tears came to Luka's eyes. "This is all my fault," he said. "Everything: Ellie, Hazel, you. And I've been terrible to Max since he got here. I'm sorry. I'm so sorry, I didn't mean for—none of this was meant to happen. But I have to save my sister. *We* have to save her! I don't deserve your help, any of you—but I can't do this on my own. I need you, *all* of you. I need the Wild Huntsboys!"

"The Wild Huntsboys." Jem nodded, pulling himself to his feet. "You bore that pain for your sister, and for me. I will not forget it."

"Pretty cool, Rake," said Hazel.

"I'm still in," said Max. "No doubt."

Hugo barked in Luka's room. A fighter patrol roared overhead, and the house shook beneath their feet.

Luka nodded. "We hardly have any time now," he said. "The networks are down, the City is on high alert, the Wardens are looking for us, the Lost Boys will be everywhere, and now the Trenchcoats have marked us. We might get beaten up, arrested, or worse. We somehow need to gather three days' worth of iron by midnight or Elena will be lost forever." He sighed deeply. "It's not going to be easy. It might be impossible."

Hazel shrugged. "What does *impossible* mean anyway?"

"It means it can't be done," replied Max. "Like, there's no way you can possibly do that thing."

"*Thank* you, Muscles," said Hazel. "I just meant—"

"Are we ready?" interrupted Jem, brushing down his coat.

"Better believe we are," said Luka, meeting the eyes of his friends in turn. "Let's do this."

36

"I don't know why you're making fun of me," said Max, joining the others in Luka's garden. "It's normal to be scared of crypts. Even in the daytime."

Hazel handed out their night-vision goggles. "It'll be dark soon enough—and it's always dark underground."

"Great," said Max. "That makes me feel *much* better. Why don't we go for the train station? Loads of iron, but no ghosts."

The garden was filled with the half-light of early evening, its colors leaching with the fading sun. There were no shadows across their faces anymore, just the soft shade of the trees.

"The Necropolis is where the oldest, strongest iron is," said Hazel, pointing at the spires between the sky-towers. "Right, Jem?"

Jem shuddered.

"Without question. Cut from the earth's black heart."

"Great, said Luka. "And there's no way we'll make it back before curfew. I wonder what the Domestic will do when he finds we're not here."

"Option one," said Hazel, chewing a strip of boiled magpie, "he feels a bit sad, so goes home to cheer himself up with a slice of cake and an herbal tea. Option two: he kicks down the door, ransacks the house, then goes on a rampage until he finds us."

"Option two seems more likely, knowing our luck," Luka muttered.

Hazel zipped up his duffel bag. "Didn't seem like an herbal tea man, did he?"

Luka saw Max chewing.

"You eat magpie now, too?"

Max nodded.

"It's all right, actually. Tastes like chicken."

"Are you planning to wear those ridiculous goggles again?" said Jem. He was running his hand along the bridge of Hugo's nose, making the dog's hind leg tremble.

"We have to," said Luka. "We can't all see in the dark, you know."

Jem rubbed Hugo harder, and laughed. "I'll never know how humans cope—how you manage to be so brave when you're so *fragile*. Are you wearing those silly face masks, too?"

"You mean the sport socks?" said Hazel, holding up his uneven ski mask. "Well, yeah. Otherwise people will know who we are."

"A mask is more than a disguise, it's a new identity.

A chance to be who you wish to be. The Junkyard Knight understands that well enough. As do I," Jem added, slipping his own mask over his head.

"We can still tell it's you," said Luka. "You're the only one who's eight inches tall."

"Such a razor wit," said Jem, inclining his head. "You should have proper masks. Masks that speak to your identity."

"And what's that?"

"Why, the Wild Huntsboys, of course. Rake, Brains, and Muscles."

"Yeah, Rake 'cause I'm skinny. How come they get cool code names?"

"Would you have a garden rake in that shed yonder?"

"He means 'over there,'" said Hazel.

"I know what it—hang on . . ." Luka headed toward what had been his dad's shed. Now it was full of summer toys and broken things: a paddling pool folded around unstable deck chairs; bikes and balls and a three-wheeled skateboard. There were bags of cement gone hard as tombstones, and the oily smell of his dad's tools. Everything was cold and gray, covered in dust and time.

"There we are," said Jem, pulling on a wooden pole twenty times his height. "This *is* a rake, isn't it?"

"That's a broom," said Luka, swapping the handles. "This is a rake."

"Aha! And look, it's even zinc-coated—how considerate," said Jem. He tossed the handle in the air, grabbed the head, and pulled. "There you go."

Luka turned the rake head over in his hands. "Thanks?"

"We're not done yet . . ." Jem laughed. He jumped on top of Luka's head, took the lump of metal from his hands, and twisted it like a marshmallow.

Luka turned to face the other Huntsboys. The rake had been bent around his head, its prongs forming a visor that hid his eyes and the top half of his face, leaving only his mouth and chin exposed.

"Ooh," said Hazel, appearing with Max in the doorway. "That's cool."

Hugo barked and backed away, then came forward with an uncertain wag.

"What am I, Rake Man?"

"Just Rake," said Hazel. He gripped Max's shoulder. "Anything in there for Muscles?"

Max pulled an old sweatband from a shelf and wiped away the cobwebs. Then, taking a box cutter from the tool rack, he cut two eyeholes and slipped it over his head. "This look okay?"

"That's exactly how it looks," said Jem.

"What about you, Brains?" said Luka.

"Tricky one . . ." said Hazel, rummaging in an old tea chest. He threw a roller skate over his shoulder, followed by a bag of paintbrushes and a broken

Weedwhacker. "I guess maybe—hey! Oh, this'll do nicely."

He pulled something over his head and turned around, pointing a Sharpie in the air like a sword.

"Why do you look so surprised?" said Jem.

"It's the swim cap," Hazel said. "It's got my eyebrows. Muscles, the box cutter, if you please."

"You want me to cut you some eyeholes?" said Max, stepping forward with the knife in his hand.

"Whoa! I think I'll take it off my head first. Just give it here." He dropped the cap to the floor, rolled up his boilersuit sleeves, and made two incisions.

"You know, Brains, we kind of need to get going," said Luka. "This *is* a kind of life-or-death thing."

"Oh, no," said Hazel, scribbling with the pen. "There's no way I'm going to be the only Huntsboy without a deadly mask. The only two-legged Huntsboy," he added, when Hugo barked.

"So, what have you—"

"There!" said Hazel, slipping the cap over his head and leaping to his feet. "What do you think?"

"You look smaller without your hair," said Max.

"And your eyes look crazy. Er—craz*ier*," added Luka. "What's with the Sharpie squiggles?"

Hazel, the swimming cap pulled down to the tip of his nose, threw his hands in the air. "It's supposed to look like a brain. Like, Brains, you know? It's my brain."

"It looks like a jellyfish," said Max.

"Or a squished-up spider," added Luka.

"Ignore them," said Jem. "You have chosen your identities. Now we're ready."

"Almost," said Hazel. "I've got something for you, too." He unzipped his giant bag.

"I figured this might come in handy. Here, I found it on the roof. Now you've got your own little teleportation shadow—can't fit an oak tree in your pocket, can you?"

Jem stared at the tiny toadstool, then looked up. "They're hard to find in winter. Thank you."

The doorbell rang on the other side of the house, and before Luka could grab his collar, Hugo barked and leaped against the back door.

"Hello?" called a deep voice.

"It's the Domestic!" hissed Luka. "He's early!"

Jem closed his eyes. "There are several human lifeforms on the other side of the building."

"He's brought his friends," said Hazel. "Time to go, I think."

"Hoi!" shouted the Domestic Warden. He barreled round the side of the house and kicked the gate open— then flinched as it rebounded in his face.

"Go!" Luka shouted.

The Huntsboys vanished into the park and headed for the Necropolis, half a dozen furious Wardens shouting curses at their backs.

37

"I'm starting to think Max might have a point," said Luka, peering at the massed ranks of gravestones. "This is pretty freaky."

He was huddled beside the others in a stairwell of lichen and moss, watching Hazel fiddling with an ancient gate.

"Well," Hazel grunted, peering inside the heavy padlock. "Remember, the crypts are full of iron—"

"And how," said Jem. "I can feel it through my suit."

Luka thought of Elena, suffering under the mark of the fairfolk, weakened further with each passing moment. "What does it feel like?"

Jem opened his mouth, then saw the question within the question.

"It doesn't hurt," he said gently, gripping his collar.

"Oh," said Luka, relieved, "I thought—" He saw the smoke sneaking through Jem's fingers. "Right. Keep working, Brains."

"Nearly there," said Hazel. "Second, we'll get *old* iron in here. No alloys or fancy new metals, like the tailfin—just solid lumps of iron, dug out of the ground hundreds of years ago and used to build the Old Town."

"How much difference does that make?" said Max.

"Quite a bit, I imagine," said Hazel, turning a pin with a *clunk*. "It must be stronger before you add the other stuff . . . like Kool-Aid without the water! Right, Jem?"

"I have no idea what 'coolade' is, but yes," said Jem. "We don't come to places like this very often; they've got layers of the very protection you seek. There's a reason Brains found these handcuffs in a crypt; old magic lives here, from when humans respected the lore. Look at these gates—pure, solid iron. I couldn't get through these without your help."

"But you'd fit through the bars," said Luka.

Jem shook his head.

"I couldn't pass through if you weren't carrying me. *That's* the power of *old* protection like this."

"Third," said Hazel, with a twist and *clunk*, "there's zero security here. Look—we've got the place to ourselves."

Luka scanned the dusky graveyard through his rake mask. It was peaceful and still, the rumble of the City seeming far away as it wove through the skeletal branches and hanging fronds. The headstones grinned oddly, pushed by the mossy, swollen ground.

He thought of his dad, lying in the North's frozen soil, below a rough-cut headstone and a City flag.

"Maybe the Wardens think no one would be evil enough to rob graves," he said.

Hazel turned around. "We're not robbing the *graves*. Jeez, is that what you thought?"

Luka glanced at Max, who nodded. "Well, yeah?"

"No! We're taking the iron from the gates and hinges and things—not the actual coffins. You must think I'm off my head!" Hazel laughed, then stopped. "How come no one else is laughing at that?"

"Just keep at the lock," said Jem. "I can feel the pins moving."

A bird called behind them. Luka turned to see a crow wafting on a thin branch, its black eyes flashing. Another joined it, and they called to each other.

"They're watching us, aren't they?"

Jem turned and saw the pine fronds clutched in the crows' feet, and spat on the ground. "Rudge," he said. "I might have known."

"Who's Rudge?"

"My enemy. And yours."

"There!" said Hazel, catching the lock before it hit the ground. "That goes in the bag—we'll hang that on the front door. Good plan, Jem?"

"Undoubtedly. I'd be unable to pass through any portal hung with this horrid thing."

"They're called doors," said Max.

They edged into the crypt. Luka stared into its darkness as Hugo sniffed around the doorway. The air inside was dusty and old, like the breath of some ancient creature. He wondered how Hazel's lock-pins had sounded, down in its depths. Like the tapping of a beak on a window, he imagined. Insistent.

And loud.

"I'm not sure about this," he said.

"If you're worried about ghosts, Rakey," said Hazel, "then don't be. They mostly come at night." He thought for a moment, then added, "Mostly."

The four of them looked ahead. The darkness intensified as the tunnel went on, deepening to a pool of ink-like, solid black.

"Still," said Max.

Hazel took a deep breath, then pulled a map from his pants.

"This is the layout inside," he said, taking a few tentative steps. "We need to get a lot of good stuff here, Huntsboys. There are only a few hours left until the Reckoning, and we need iron on every window and every door. We've got the padlock, but that still leaves eight pieces of good iron to collect."

"We're going to make it," said Luka. "I know we are. And I'm glad you're with me. All of you."

He nodded at Hazel, then turned to Max—but found only empty space.

"Hey!" he said. "Where's—"

Max cleared his throat. The other Huntsboys turned to see him standing in a puddle of light that spilled through a hole in the tunnel's roof.

"If anything happens," Max said, his voice

wavering, "I want you to know . . . that scar . . . I delivered messages for resistance fighters. Paper. No phones—no trail. One day they caught me, so I ran. But they got me anyway." He made a shooting gesture with his hand. "I thought I had torn in two. There was so much blood. When I was in the hospital, my house was hit by the bomb."

"That killed your parents?" said Luka.

Max nodded. "I thought you should know. Someone should know what I've done, what's happened to me, in case, you know—"

Luka nodded, and gripped his hand. "We're going to make it," he said again.

Hazel coughed.

"Oh, all right," said Luka, and took his hand too. Hugo nosed in between them, and Jem settled on the dog's broad head.

The Huntsboys held hands in the dark, watching the drones' light blink through the clouds.

"Got your night vision ready?" said Hazel.

They clicked their goggles, which glowed into life. Luka saw the path ahead for the first time—flagstones and earth, winding beneath a low ceiling.

"Imagine needing *machines* to see in the dark," said Jem. "How you creatures evolved into a dominant species really is astounding."

Luka stepped to the front and palmed his coin.

"Follow me," he said.

38

The air on their faces changed as soon as they were below the ground—a warm breeze that tasted of history and mud.

"Take a left, Rake," said Hazel, peering at the map.

"Can't we use the visualizer?" said Luka.

"This far underground? No, we can't. Or anything else. Besides, ghosts wouldn't show up on it anyway, remember?"

"Ha ha," said Max.

A forked junction appeared in Luka's grainy vision. When he turned to follow Hazel's directions his foot slipped on unseen water, and he plunged his hand into the soft wall.

"Yuck," he whispered, wiping it on his jeans. "What's this place made of?"

"Dirt," said Jem. "The City is built on clay. Can't you smell it? Sort of . . . clean. Like a pebble."

They all sniffed.

"It smells old," said Max.

"It is," said Jem quietly.

Luka glanced down. The faerie was pressed flat against Hugo's head, his eyes shining.

"You all right?" he said.

Jem nodded, but said nothing.

They walked a few minutes in silence, only the directions from Hazel puncturing the sound of their feet and the constant, soft trickle of water as they moved deeper into the earth.

Luka stopped abruptly, and Max ran into him.

"What?" he said.

Luka pointed wordlessly.

Set into a huge shelf on the wall, as neat as a baker's window, were stacks of cobwebbed bones, studded with hollow, toothy skulls.

"We're here," whispered Hazel. "There should be lots of good stuff around here, if we—"

"This doesn't freak you out?" said Luka, eyes fixed on the staring sockets of the nearest skull.

"What? Those? No . . . should it? Look, this is what I'm talking about." Hazel ran his hands along the wall. "This hook is for an old torch, and—"

"Brains . . ." said Max.

"—it's pure iron! If you take the big pliers and—"

"*Hazel!*" hissed Max. "How many people are buried here?"

Hazel paused, hands deep in the bag on Max's back. "Why?"

"I just . . . I want to know."

"All right. One million seven hundred and eighty-five thousand. And six."

Max spluttered as the air left his chest. "A

million—" he said, placing his hand on his heart. "You serious?"

"Yeah," said Hazel, bending to peer into a nose cavity. "Three hundred years ago they started emptying the cemeteries because they were too full after, like, a thousand years of plague and stuff—"

"Plague?" said Luka, dropping his face in his hands.

"—then the walls of the Southern Graveyard collapsed, and all the bodies spilled into—"

"Enough," said Luka, patting Max on the back. "Just go back to that thing on the wall."

Hazel shrugged and hefted his pliers. The bolts each gave way after three stiff turns, and the hook fell to the ground.

Max caught it and tested a magnet on its surface. The magnet leaped forward like a startled cat, locking onto the hook's surface.

"It's heavy," he said.

Jem covered his mouth, nausea crossing his face.

"By the lore itself, that thing is pure poison," he said. "Put it away, please."

Hazel dropped the hook in the bag, then went back to the wall. Luka took his own pliers and they worked in tandem, removing another piece of ancient metal from the wooden beams of the crypt, then another, and another, the bag on Max's back growing heavier as it filled with iron. Hugo paced around, sniffing at the bones and licking the water from the walls.

"That's eight pieces!" said Hazel, wiping his brow and crouching beside what looked like an old fireplace. "What about this grate? Should we take it?"

Luka stepped closer to get a better look. "It's pretty big. Maybe we could put it across the back door."

"And who do you think's going to carry it?" said Max.

"Now, now, Muscles, you know the answer to that," said Hazel.

Luka locked his hands on one of the iron struts and dug his heels in the ground. "It looks good to me. Give me a hand with it."

"I think I'll pass," said Jem, fanning his sweating face.

Hazel crouched beside Luka, and Max took hold of the far end. Luka felt Hugo bite the waistband of his jeans.

"We ready? One, two, three!"

The Huntsboys gritted their teeth and pulled as hard as they could when a flailing skeleton, bound only by shreds of decayed clothing, tumbled from the wall and landed on Luka, its skull screaming wide-mouthed into his face.

"Aaaaargh!" he yelled, trying to roll away but simply spinning with the corpse like an Olympic wrestler.

"Rake!" shouted Hazel, grabbing Luka's shoulders. "Hold still!"

"It's got me!" shouted Luka. "It's got me!"

Hugo tugged his sleeve and Jem pushed the skull away from his face until, finally, the bones stopped moving and Max lifted him to his feet.

Hands on his knees, gasping for breath, Luka looked at the other Huntboys—and burst out laughing.

"Jeez, Rake!" said Hazel. "Your face!"

"*My* face?" said Luka. "Too bloody right 'my face'! I thought that was it!"

Max looked serious. "Maybe we should go. We could bring a curse on ourselves."

"Another one?" said Hazel. "Here, this thing's nearly off, one more pull should do it." He grabbed the grate and tugged.

An enormous groan echoed through the tunnel.

The Huntsboys froze.

"We all heard that, right?" said Luka.

Hugo growled in his chest, and Jem smoothed his fur.

"Should I try again?" whispered Hazel.

"No," said Max.

"Yes," said Luka carefully, his heart pounding. "We need it. For Ellie. Let's have one more go."

Hazel fixed his hands in place, nodded to the others, and pulled.

A huge wave of sound washed over them, like a belch from the stomach of the world, and Hazel fell to the ground.

The Huntsboys looked around frantically and strained their ears, gripping each other's arms and huddling close together.

"Jem," said Luka, "do you recognize that sound?"

"In a human grave site? No, I—"

"I mean could it be, like, a monster or something?"

"Oh." Jem thought for a moment. "I suppose so. Yes."

"Come *on*," said Max. "Let's go, now—"

"Wait!" hissed Luka, waving his hands for silence. Nothing happened.

"Rake—"

"Shh! *Listen.*"

A voice, tiny and far-off, whistled through the tunnel . . . followed by a laugh.

"We're not alone," said Luka. "And I know that laugh."

He ran deeper into the crypt, the walls flashing past in a blurry, night-vision glow. He heard the others keeping pace as light swelled ahead and he tore off his goggles, letting his naked eyes look upon the hidden world of the dead for the first time.

A huge room, twice the size of his school's gym, loomed before him. It was filled with pyramids of grinning skulls, its walls crisscrossed with bones. And there, as Luka had known he would be, was the Junkyard Knight, arms raised in triumph atop one of the macabre piles. His Lost Boys scurried behind their torchlit phones, gathering the bolts and hinges for which the Huntsboys had come.

"That's *our* iron," Luka said as the others gathered behind him. Jem slipped into his sleeve.

"So, what's the plan, Rake?" said Hazel.

Luka shrugged.

"Get it back," he said—and charged.

39

"There he is!" shouted the Junkyard Knight. "And he's *masked*! Oh, Lucky Luka, we *knew* you'd come! This is the best iron in the City, but the Government is too scared to take it."

"He's not daft, this lad," said Hazel approvingly. "Great minds and all that."

The Junkyard Knight hopped to the ground and walked toward them.

"We're not scared," he said, showing the deep cut on his forearm. "Not the Lost Boys. And not *you*! So, Luka, I ask one last time: Will you *join* us? Will you swear the oath and make the mark? Will you make the cut and add your blood to ours? Then you can have all the scrap your heart desires."

Luka took a step forward. He rolled up his sleeves.

"What are you doing?" hissed Jem, his face exposed to the light.

The Junkyard Knight nodded. "This is a good decision, child. A *good* decision."

"What are you doing?" echoed Max urgently. "Stay with us!"

"Are you kidding?" said Luka. "Join *this* guy? I just wanted to give him the message as clearly as I could, seeing as he doesn't seem to have gotten it already."

And he gave the Junkyard Knight, his rusting mask cast long in the shadow of his flaming torch, a clear, unambiguous hand signal.

The Huntsboys exploded with laughter.

The Knight's shoulders dropped. "Bad move," he said.

He dropped his torch in a puddle at his feet. Darkness flooded the space.

The Lost Boys lowered their weapons.

"Goggles on," hissed Hazel.

The Junkyard Knight began to thrash the ground with his bat in a terrible, echoing rhythm. Luka heard movement around him in the dark—the hair-prickling sound of lots of people making absolutely no noise.

He fumbled his night vision on and, as the grainy image whirred into life, he saw why the Knight had laughed, and just who had been moving so silently.

The pillars of skulls were crawling with Lost Boys. Scores of them, *hundreds* of them; some in masks, some with their faces simply hidden behind taped cardboard. All of them carried weapons.

And all of them were staring directly at him.

There was a flare in the darkness, and the Junkyard Knight relit his flaming torch.

"This is the boy who was too good to be lost!" he shouted, banging the ground.

The Lost Boys banged their weapons, once, in

response. The sound was enormous, like the heartbeat of a God, and the silence after rang with its hostile intent.

"This is the boy who, with his mangy dog, defiled our home!" shouted the Knight.

Another crash of thunder.

Hugo barked and bared his teeth. Luka grabbed the Huntsboys' sleeves and began to back away, toward the tunnel, picking up pace.

"Maybe I shouldn't have done that," he said.

"You're probably right," said Hazel. "Seeing as how there's hundreds of them and five of us."

The Lost Boys raised their weapons—and rushed forward.

"Retreat!" shouted Jem.

The Huntsboys bolted back into the tunnel, the glowing shapes of bones and skulls flashing past their goggles. Luka started to fall behind, his weak leg deadening as fatigue started to settle into his muscles, and he felt the ground tremble below the Lost Boys' feet.

"Grab him!" shouted the Junkyard Knight, his bat thudding against the walls.

Max grabbed Luka's shoulder and hauled him forward, and together they stumbled over the fallen skeleton they'd pulled from the grate.

"We don't have everything we need yet!" Luka shouted.

"No time!" panted Hazel, picking up pace as the

gates loomed ahead, lit by rods of moonlight. "We only need one more good-sized piece of iron! We'll go to the train station, and if that doesn't work we'll—"

"You'll what?" said a deep voice.

The Trenchcoat dropped into the stairwell, blocking the Huntsboys' exit. Torches flared in the darkness around him, their light making bright coins of his glasses. "Where's my missing tailfin?" he growled.

The Huntsboys stopped, skidding on the soggy floor and clattering together.

Behind them, the Lost Boys' footsteps beat closer, punctuated by the snare drum of their bats on the walls.

"What do we do?" hissed Max.

"There's only one thing we can do," said Jem.

"Is it something crazy?" said Hazel.

Luka heard the rasp of a Lost Boy's breath over his shoulder.

"Keep going!" he shouted, surging forward.

The Trenchcoat braced himself, arms at his sides. More bespectacled faces appeared behind him.

"Cover your ears!" yelled Jem.

"What?" said Hazel.

"*Now!*"

The Huntsboys clapped their hands over their ears as the faerie opened his mouth—and *kept* opening it, his jaw distending like a snake's as his teeth unfurled behind his lips.

He screamed, a piercing shriek that Luka felt even behind his tight-pressed hands, the sound shaking his bones and fizzing his blood.

He looked ahead and saw the Trenchcoat drop to his knees, a trickle of blood seeping from his ears and nose, his glasses pulled across his nose by his desperate hands.

"Keep going!" Luka shouted, knowing it was pointless, that nothing could possibly be heard over Jem's cry, and as Hazel vaulted over the prone figure of the Trenchcoat, he looked back into the tunnel to see the Lost Boys scattered on the ground. Those who could walk were vanishing back into the crypt, their bats forgotten as they gripped their skulls in blistering pain.

Jem closed his mouth.

"Did it work?" he asked.

Luka, last to leave the tunnel, turned back.

"I'd say so."

He pushed Hugo up the steps and lifted his leg to step over the Trenchcoat, when the man's hand shot out and grabbed his ankle.

"You don't understand," the agent said, all his bluster stripped away. "It's an *emergency*. The peace we've been seeking, the promise we've made . . . lost, if we don't secure that wreckage. *All* of it."

"But I need it," said Luka. "My sister, she's sick. If I don't—"

The Trenchcoat's eyes began to roll into his head.

"You need to do the right thing," he whispered. "I'll be on the bridge. Look for the nodes . . . pull the tail . . ."

"We'd best go," said Jem, tugging Luka's ear.

"Come on, Rake!" shouted Hazel, somewhere in the graveyard's evening shadow.

"What was he talking about? Did he say 'pull the tail'?" said Luka as he sprinted up the steps, hopscotching between the stricken bodies of the assembled Trenchcoats and away from the Necropolis.

"Who knows?" said Jem. "I can't understand what humans are on about half the time. Just keep moving."

40

They didn't slow until they'd reached Wildwood Park and exhaustion had left their lungs empty and cold. Hazel checked the visualizer for any dots following them, but it was empty.

"We're all right," he said. "We lost them."

"What was that noise?" said Luka.

Jem puffed out his chest. "Did you like it?"

"I mean . . . no, it was horrific. But it worked."

Max was looking back the way they'd come, his chest heaving with the effort of carrying the crypt's iron.

"Check the scanner," he said. "Make sure there's no one nearby."

"Good call," said Luka. "Maybe we can sneak into the station by the entrance on North Street. There must be *something* there we can cart off without too much trouble."

Hazel slipped his AirPod into his ear and set to twisting the dials on his watch.

"They're looking for us," he said. "Oh, like, looking for us a *lot*. A lot a lot. They've sent out a couple of patrols. And—hang on."

"What?" said Luka. A drone whirred overhead, hidden in the gloom.

"It's an *enemy frequency*," hissed Hazel, eyes widening.

The others gathered round.

"Have you hacked into one of those before?" said Luka.

"Shh! They're talking about a new weapon. A chemical weapon."

Luka's body seized, and the world seemed to slow around him. "A chemical attack?" he said. "Here?"

Hazel nodded. "It's going to be dropped on the City at dawn, in revenge for . . ." He hammered a button on his watch. "There's too much static—the broken promise?"

"The Trenchcoat," Luka said, his heart skipping. "He said the peace would be lost without *all* of the wreckage. He said they'd made a promise! This is what he was talking about! They need that tailfin to keep their promise to the Enemy, or they'll launch a chemical attack!"

"*Oh,*" said Max, his mouth wide. "But *we* need it. We've already sliced it up on the windowsills!"

Jem gripped Luka's hair as he knuckled his closed eyes. Spots flashed in his vision. "The whole City could be wiped out in a chemical attack," he said.

"We won't have enough iron if we take it back!" said

Hazel. "The Reckoning is at *midnight*! They'll kill us!"

"I know, Hazel—"

"And they'll take Elena. Rake, we can't—"

"I *know*, Hazel! But the *whole* City! Everyone! Millions of people dead, because of us! We have to take it in!"

Hazel looked at Max. "What do you think?"

"We're dead either way," said Max.

"So, we do the right thing," said Luka.

"But your sister's not *in* the City," said Hazel. "We could save her."

Luka felt a lurch in his stomach.

"What do you think, Jem?" he said. "What should we do?"

"What else is leadership but making the tough decisions?" said the faerie, patting Luka's head.

Luka looked at his friends, faces slack with worry under their Huntsboy masks. Hugo nudged his leg, and he pulled the dog's big head against him, closing his eyes as he palmed his coin.

"Heads, we take it in," he said. "That's what Elena would say—what she would want me to say."

The coin caught the moonlight as it spun, flashing white at its apex before snapping back into Luka's hand.

He unfolded his fingers.

"Heads it is," said Hazel. "I can't believe you left that to chance, Rake."

Luka turned the coin over, showing another head on the other side. "I didn't. We can't risk so many people's lives to save our own. We're taking the tailfin to the Trenchcoat."

The others sighed.

"So, death by faeries?" said Hazel.

"I'll have something to say when the Reckoning comes," said Jem, drawing his sword, the blade reflecting a galaxy of stars as it turned.

"I can't ask you to do that," said Luka. "Not for us. You've done more than enough, and—"

"That's plenty," said Jem, holding up his hand. "I'll hear no more protest."

Luka went to palm his coin—but held out his hand to the others instead.

"We go together," he said. "But they're not going to arrest us. I promise."

"They're not?" said Max.

"Nope," said Luka, squeezing their hands. "I've got a plan."

41

The bridge was empty, its cobblestones gleaming like snakeskin.

Hazel and Max wobbled along behind Luka, the tailfin held between them, bound crudely by duct tape.

"All the other bridges are in the New Town," said Hazel, nervously chewing another strip of magpie. "This is the last one, and there's nobody here."

Luka stared at the visualizer. Except for their own dots blinking at the center, it was completely empty. "He said he'd be 'on the bridge.' I don't get it! Why would he lie when he wants this back so badly?"

Hazel dropped the tailfin and scratched under his swimming-cap mask.

"Maybe he's just messing with us."

"He wouldn't do that though, would he? And you're the one who heard the transmission about the chemical bombs. Do you think that was made up just to mess with us?"

"No," said Hazel, "I guess not."

Luka leaned against the wall and grabbed his head. A statue above cast a long, jagged shadow across the road, its lines wobbling over the cobblestones.

"He said something else . . . What *was* it? 'Look

for . . . the nodes,' and . . . 'pull the tail'! Pull the tail!"

The others looked blank.

"What are you talking about, Rake?" said Hazel. "The world is about to break into a chemical apocalypse and you're talking in riddles?"

Luka paced back and forth, scanning the paving slabs.

"But that's what the Trenchcoat said! Look for something that could be a tail, it might be one of the coats of arms, or a crack in the sidewalk, or—"

"Could it be that statue of a dog?" said Jem, pointing over Luka's head.

They all looked up.

"That'll do it," said Luka.

"Rake!" said Hazel, heaving the tailfin back onto his shoulder and crossing the road with Max. "He didn't say *nodes*, that's *Nodens*. If you'd said *that* then I—" He looked at their blank expressions. "Nobody else? Oh, come *on*! Nodens! Ancient God of hunting and dogs! We should have guessed, really—he's like the Huntboys' patron saint."

Luka gazed up at the statue's stoic face. The God was facing forward, staring into the future, his hand pressed to the head of a great, strong hound.

Hugo nosed his hand, and Luka ruffled his ears. "Ready?" he said—and pulled the statue-dog's tail.

The hound's eyes lit up red and a panel slid aside in the bridge wall, revealing a hidden door.

"All *right*," said Hazel, clapping his hands together. "I *knew* there was stuff like this somewhere! Proper spy stuff!"

The Huntboys looked at the door that had appeared. It was made from the same marble as the wall, and its surface appeared to be completely smooth.

"Is there a bell?" said Luka.

As he stepped forward a voice hissed through an unseen speaker.

"Name?"

Luka jumped back. "Um . . . Rake."

There was a pause. The speaker seemed to be thinking.

"Real name?"

"That is my real name," said Luka. "As far as you're concerned. Because if you want this . . ."

He signaled to Hazel and Max, who waggled the tailfin and smiled.

There was another pause—then the door buzzed open, revealing a dim-lit staircase of spiral stone.

"Just my sort of place," said Jem.

"Huntsboys"—Luka grinned as Hugo sprinted down the steps—"let's turn ourselves in."

42

"You!" Luka shouted, as the Trenchcoat walked into the small, white room to which the Huntsboys had been led.

The room was cold, its walls and floor made of shining concrete, and the man's clipped shoes echoed in the small space.

"We have something to tell you!" Luka went on. "We heard a—"

The Trenchcoat—tall, with neatly clipped hair and beads of sweat in his moustache—raised a hand and settled across the table, fixing them with his bespectacled stare.

"My ears have just about stopped ringing," he said, unbuttoning his coat. "Would you mind telling me what kind of sonic weapon was able to disable so many of my men?"

"But it's about—"

"I will control this conversation, or you will be separated and questioned individually. Now. Tell me about your weapon."

Luka stared at his own image, reflected in the man's extraordinary glasses. Then he turned to Hazel and Max. "What do you think?"

"In for a penny," said Hazel, shrugging.

Max nodded.

Luka placed his arm on the plastic tabletop.

"Come on out, Jem."

The faerie hauled himself from Luka's coat sleeve, shaking his hair as he stood grinning up at the Trenchcoat with his sharp little teeth.

"Evening, Officer," he said.

"I see," said the Trenchcoat, his expression hardly moving. After some thought, he appeared to reach a conclusion, his brow unfurrowed, and he smiled. "You need not call me 'Officer.' Call me Mr. Clarke. I am not a policeman, nor am I a soldier."

"What are you?" said Hazel.

"I am a . . . functionary of the state."

"You mean the Government?" said Luka.

The Trenchcoat took a sip of water and shook his head. "We are beyond Government. Elected politicians change, but we remain. We are in the shadow of every action, every consequence. As the world ticks, gentlemen, we are the tock. But that nearly came to an end when you stole my tailfin."

He gestured to the corner of the room, where the tailfin leaned against the wall. Luka saw the damage done by the band saw, inadequately hidden by strips of tape.

"We're sorry," he said. "We needed it for help with . . . a fight. Against the faerie world."

Clarke took another sip and took off his glasses, revealing tired, bloodshot eyes.

Kind eyes—like Dad's, Luka thought.

"Five minutes ago I'd have laughed you out of this room, but when presented with the evidence"—Clarke nodded at Jem—"I can hardly deny that seems entirely plausible. I don't understand, though—why take a piece from an aircraft to deal with faeries?"

"It just had to be iron," said Hazel. "They hate iron. And when the plane went down, we . . . thought it might help us."

Clarke nodded. "I see. Well, it contains some iron—it's made from a complex alloy, but it's there. We've been having a little problem with some young men stealing scrap metal, as it happens, which is why I foolishly allowed the plane to stay in the marsh for so long."

"I knew there was something weird going on!" Luka gasped, punching Hazel on the leg. "It *was* a trap!"

Clarke nodded. "But not for you."

"The Junkyard Knight," said Max.

Clarke laughed. "I suppose so. We call him Rusty. That was his nickname, before he put on the mask. His real name is Russell Hanratty—a perfectly ordinary young man who turned from the right path a long time ago. He's created something of a mystique around himself. That mask . . . but he's not as fearsome as he seems. I have it on good authority that he still sleeps with a teddy called 'Sunshine Bubbles.'"

"Oh, isn't that just super?" said Hazel.

"Quite. In any case, he and his Lost Boys have become something of a . . . thorn in my side. I knew they'd rush to that plane if we broadcast its position. Imagine my surprise when you four appeared, too."

Hugo barked and pawed Clarke's leg.

"What does your dog want?" he said.

"He's one of us, too," said Luka. "There are five Huntsboys—human, faerie, and dog."

"And you've joined Rusty's little gang, have you?"

"What?" said Luka. "Oh, the masks? No! These are ours. We would never have anything to do with him. But listen, if you needed that plane so badly, wasn't it a bit stupid to use it as bait?"

Clarke finished his water and dabbed his lips.

"That's a very polite phrasing of the question my superiors have been asking since I returned with an incomplete wreckage. Missing, of all things, the most important part."

Hazel nodded.

"The insignia," he said.

Clarke frowned.

"Yes," he said. "Now, normally you'd find—"

"Yeah, yeah," said Hazel. "It's missing the mission design series. What else?"

Clarke raised his eyebrows. "What incredible technical knowledge. You must be the boy from the old watchtower," he said as Hazel flushed. "Yes, there is no mission design series. This aircraft represents our most advanced capabilities—completely classified, of course—and it was to be a gift for the Enemy, who had been sending an agent carrying *their* most classified weapon. By sharing our technology, we hoped to demonstrate our willingness to cooperate, and our desire to de-escalate the hostilities that have existed for much of your lifetimes."

They looked at each other across the empty table.

"You wanted to stop the War," said Luka. "And you were going to give them this to prove it."

"Beautifully put," said Clarke. "Without the unmarked tailfin, of course, we couldn't demonstrate the plane's top-secret nature, thereby nullifying the entire gesture. The Enemy took its nonappearance as a betrayal of trust. We don't know how they'll respond, but—"

"We do!" said Luka, standing so quickly he knocked his chair against the wall. "That's what I was trying to tell you! Hazel overheard an Enemy message—they're planning a chemical attack on the City at dawn! That's why we brought the tailfin back."

Clarke sat up. "When did you hear this?"

"An hour ago," said Hazel. "Maybe a little more."

"And you're in no doubt that was the nature of the communication?"

"It was a bit staticky, but it was clear enough. It's why we're here."

Clarke looked grave. "That was the top-secret weapon they were sending in exchange: the chemical bomb. And now they're going to send it all the same."

"Only it'll explode," said Max.

"Thank you, boys," said Clarke, standing to leave. "Now, I'm afraid you'll have to stay here while we—"

"No!" shouted Luka. "You have to let us go!"

"I'm afraid that's impossible." Clarke fastened his coat and slipped on his glasses. "You've broken so many laws that even if I—"

"But the faeries are coming at midnight," said Luka. "My sister, she's in danger! We need to get back to my house and make sure it's protected, or I'll lose her forever, and it'll be all my fault!"

Clarke looked at him, then lowered his face to Jem's.

"Is this true, sir? Are your people seeking to hurt this young man?"

Jem made a face. "It's a little more complicated than that," he said. "The lore is the lore is the lore. But the nub of it is he's in terrible danger. They all are."

Clarke straightened up and turned to go. "I'm afraid it's out of my hands."

"What if we gave you the Junkyard Knight? I know where his hideout is," said Luka. He covered his mouth, then held out the key he'd taken from the Knight's pocket. "I can give him to you."

The Trenchcoat froze in the doorway. "We've been looking for that hideout for months," he said doubtfully. "How did *you* find it?"

"He took me there," said Luka. "They tried to make me join, but I smashed the place up and escaped."

"He brought home a spanner," said Hazel.

Luka kicked him under the table.

Clarke thought for a moment, then nodded. "You deliver him to us within the hour, or I'll put out a warrant for your arrest. Deal?"

"Deal," said Luka.

Hazel hopped onto the table, then took some coffee from his pocket and smeared it on his teeth.

"Oh, we can totally do this. But we'll need a truck. No—*ten* trucks, full of Wardens. And you need to turn the data back on for us."

Clarke suppressed a smile. "You drive a hard bargain," he said. "But you need to make it count; fail to deliver and those Wardens will be after *you*."

"The Huntsboys always deliver. Right, guys?"

"Oh, yeah," said Luka, who felt things were getting out of hand.

"I'll do my best on the data," said Clarke, "but that

sort of thing is really above my pay grade. The curfew is of national importance, and even we have very little power to change it. Now, I really must go. Remember, the fate of the City hangs in the balance." He nodded to the Huntsboys, tickled Hugo under the chin, and left the room.

They sat in silence for a heartbeat. Then Hazel spoke.

"Did we just become . . . proper spies?"

Luka stood up. "I guess so."

"It's good that we've brought the tailfin back," said Max. "But what are we going to do about the iron? The house is nowhere near covered, and it's almost ten o'clock. The Reckoning is nearly here!"

Luka held out his arm. Jem ran onto his shoulder. "Our dear friend the Junkyard Knight—Rusty, I guess—has more iron than we could ever need. Let's pay him a visit, shall we?"

43

The wind whipped through Luka's hair as he leaned out from the truck, one hand gripping the doorframe as he sped below the star-filled, blackout sky.

"Get back inside, son," said the driver, grinning under his mustache and chewing his gum. "And make sure that dog doesn't pee in my cab."

Luka leaned back under the canvas and sat down. Hazel was sitting beside the driver, quizzing him on the instruments and dials.

"—and look at *this*," he was saying, holding what looked like a black cube. "I read about these, but I didn't think they'd be used on a regular *patrol vehicle*! Tell me, are these standard-issue?"

"Where am I going now?" said the driver, changing gear with a *thunk*.

"Left, left, then right," said Luka. "The old church on the bombed-out street. But don't park too close."

The driver tipped back his Warden's helmet and laughed.

"Old Clarkey's gone off his rocker this time," he said. "Taking orders from bloody kids?"

"You just keep an eye on your satnav," said Hazel. "We'll take care of the Lost Boys."

The truck slowed as they began to pass bombed-out houses, its big tires easing over scattered wreckage and broken wood. Luka leaned out the back and watched the rest of the convoy pull onto the sidewalk, their engines grumbling to a halt.

"Right," he said. "The place isn't too heavily barricaded, but that might have changed since I was last here. Stay behind me and follow my lead."

"Listen to you," said Jem, chuckling in Luka's sleeve. "Captain of the ship."

"What is it, Brains?" said Luka, seeing Hazel's face knotted in thought.

"Well, did you see them all in the crypt?"

"Yeah," said Luka. "They all ran at us with baseball bats—they were kind of hard to miss."

Hazel waved his hands and pulled at his mask. "No, before that," he said. "When they were searching for the iron. They were all using the torches on their *phones*. And what have I told you about leaving your phone switched on?"

"Not to do it?" said Max.

"Because they're so *easily* hackable," said Hazel, nodding. "What if I hack their handsets and broadcast their GPS markers to the Trenchcoats? That way, they'll all pop up at once on the Wardens' tablets, computers, satnavs, everything. It'll be like a visualizer the size of the city! The Knight *must* have his own hacked

Wi-Fi, so you just get me inside, and I'll do the rest."

The truck shuddered to a halt.

"Can't go any closer," said the driver. "Here, what are you doing to my satnav?"

"Provided old Clarkey has done what he said he'd do, the Lost Boys' locations will appear there in a few minutes," said Hazel. "There'll be a whole bunch of dots, probably running away. I'll send you all their data, and I'll mark the big fish—the Junkyard Knight himself—in red."

The driver nodded in disbelief. "Happy fishing, boys," he said as the Huntsboys scurried across the tarmac.

"Which is the main door?" whispered Hazel.

Luka pointed as they ran. "That's the one I came out of, anyway."

As they approached the door, Max slowed down.

"We can't all go," he said.

"What?" hissed Hazel. "What are you talking about? Of course we all have to go, that's the whole point!"

Max shook his head. The wind snapped across the river behind him, throwing his hair over his face. "No, we can't all walk up at once, it'll look suspicious," he said. "I'll go—you sneak in behind me. I'll keep him talking while you hack the network."

Luka and Hazel exchanged a glance.

"Are you sure?" said Luka, handing him the key.

Max nodded, then smiled. "I'm Muscles, right? What could go wrong?"

He strode forward and slipped the key into the lock.

For a moment, nothing happened. Then a tiny pinprick of light appeared in a window, followed by the silhouette of a face.

"I want to see the Knight!" shouted Max. "I want to join! To—"

"Make the cut!" hissed Luka.

"To make the cut!" Max echoed, arms spread at his sides.

"The Knight is sleeping," said the boy, his voice small inside a plastic Santa mask.

"Then I guess you'll have to wake him up now, won't you?" said Max, grabbing the boy's collar and lifting him from the ground as the rest of the Huntsboys snuck in behind.

The Lost Boy froze, unsure whether to fight back or shout for help.

"Hurry up," said Max after making sure Luka and Hazel were inside, dropping the Lost Boy and striding into the church.

Gasping for breath, the Lost Boy bolted the door with a heavy *clank* and followed Max through the towers of junk.

Luka and Hazel tiptoed through the shadows in the corners of the church, Hugo padding at their heels.

"He did well there," said Luka. "'Course, it helps when you can pick people up by the neck."

"I enjoyed that bit," agreed Jem. His voice had tightened around the iron. Luka patted his shoulder.

"Some stash of iron in here right enough," whispered Hazel, gazing up at the leaning towers. "We could cover the whole house!" He fixed his eyes on the visualizer and unfolded a small laptop from inside his boilersuit. "They're all up ahead—look."

Luka peered over his shoulder at the mass of bright dots. Two were moving through the church, side by side. "There's Max," he said. "God, I hope he's all right."

"He will be. But we're in trouble."

"How? There's no one coming."

"Because of that," said Hazel, nodding at the laptop's screen. In the corner, next to the battery indicator and the volume and the time, was a little crossed-out globe.

"There's no Wi-Fi?" said Luka. "I thought Clarke said—"

"What's the point of being a secret agent guy if you can't even get the Wi-Fi back on?" Hazel scowled, frantically hammering the buttons on his laptop.

"Is there nothing you can do?"

"How many times, Rake? It doesn't matter how off-grid you want to be, you still need the network! Without it, I can't hack into their phones, and if we can't do that, then we can't hand their locations to Clarke. He'll arrest us after all—and he knows about my tree! I'll get locked up forever!"

"Oh my God," said Luka, staring at the screen, where more and more dots were appearing. "There's hundreds of them. Max is out there on his own waiting for us to get this done!"

"Oh, no no no . . ." said Hazel, looking around frantically. "This is bad! If the data mast was close by, we could turn it on manually, but it's on Ellie's Island! Even if we had a helicopter, we'd never get there in time!"

"I might venture a proposal," said Jem.

They looked at him.

"You said Elena could turn on this . . . mast . . . manually?"

"Yes," said Hazel, "but without data or Wi-Fi we can't tell her *how* to do that, so—"

Jem reached into his pack. "Take off my handcuffs," he said, setting the toadstool on the ground, where it cast a small shadow over the concrete floor. "Set me free, and I'll jump through this shadow and be with your sister in an instant. That is, if you trust me."

Luka held Jem's eyes for a moment. "Give me the key," he said to Hazel.

"You sure about this?"

Luka turned to Jem.

"He's one of us, isn't he?" he said, holding out his hand.

Hazel handed him two keys, joined by a brass ring, one the size of a door key, the other the size of a pine needle. Luka unlocked his own wrist, then took the handcuffs from Jem.

"I should have done this before," he said.

Jem closed his eyes and rubbed his wrist. "Oh, that feels better."

"Make sure she's all right," said Luka.

"Right, the mast has a panel on it," said Hazel, "about two levels up. It's like a laptop, and you just—"

"Like a what?"

Hazel held up his computer. "One of these! You need to get this right! We can't afford to—" he shouted.

Luka clamped his hand over Hazel's mouth.

"Shh!" he hissed. "They'll hear us!"

They waited, listening. They heard the Junkyard Knight shout in the distance, drawing a roar from his followers. Then they heard Max's voice, followed by the Knight's shrill laugh.

And footsteps. Coming toward them.

"Just here," said a voice. "I heard it, I swear. Someone shouted."

Hazel grabbed Jem's hand and spoke as quickly as he could. "Take this." He held out the silver memory stick Luka had pickpocketed the previous morning.

"This flash drive contains a program, a virus, really, that'll bring the networks back on! Tell Ellie to open the Goblin File and leave everything else. All right?"

"I haven't the faintest clue what you just said!" shouted Jem, as a host of Lost Boys rushed at them from the shadows, bats raised. "I can't drive!"

"What?" said Luka. "No, a *flash* drive!" He ducked away from a swinging bat. "Go!"

"All right," said Jem, puffing out his cheeks. He bared his teeth at the onrushing Lost Boys, then, flash drive gripped across his chest, leaped into the toad-stool's shadow and disappeared.

"You—hide!" said Luka, grabbing Hazel by the hand and pocketing the toadstool as they ran. "Midnight is less than an hour away. You need to be ready when Jem and Ellie switch on the network."

Hazel saluted.

"Good luck, Rake," he said, and scrambled up a pile of junk and disappeared.

Luka clapped his hands together, throwing a puff of smoke from his sleeve behind him, blinding the on-rushing Lost Boys.

He ran toward the sound and the light, listening to the Junkyard Knight's crowing laughter and the Lost Boys' rumbles as he felt the first feathers of heat on his skin.

Rounding the final corner, he saw the fire—a mass of burning paper and wood, casting the Junkyard

Knight in an enormous, terrifying shadow.

"Rusty!" Luka shouted. "It's time to give up—you're surrounded! It's over!"

Silence filled the church. Max, who had been shoved to his knees, turned, his eye blacked and swollen.

The Junkyard Knight cocked his head and laughed. "Rusty? That name died when I put on the mask. You know what I'm talking about—Muscles here has told us everything. Look at you. *Rake*. When we brought you here you were just *Luka*. You were scared. Weak! Now look what we've turned you into!"

Luka shook his head. "I'm the same person I was before, and so are the rest of you. You don't need to follow him," he said, addressing the Lost Boys. "There are truckloads of Wardens waiting for you outside. Rusty doesn't care about you. Come with us and be safe!"

"No," said the Junkyard Knight. He lifted two torches from the bonfire and spun them in his hands. "We are lost. We are the *Lost Boys*. There is no safety for us, not anymore!"

He pointed the torches and ran at Luka, ribbons of flame streaking behind him, his eyes wide and black and pitiless.

Luka screamed and rushed forward, kicking up more puffs of smoke from his sleeves. But as the Knight swung through the clouds, suddenly Max was there, his huge arms deflecting the blow that was destined for Luka's unguarded neck, bringing it into the side of his own head.

"No!" shouted Luka as Max fell. He covered Max's prone body with his own, tearing off his mask and patting his face. "Max! Max!"

"It's over," said the Junkyard Knight, looming over him. "No one refuses the oath."

He raised the burning clubs and swung.

44

Elena stared into the darkness. She'd thought she'd known darkness during the blackouts in Bellum, but the Islands had a night all of their own. It was so thick you could feel it on your skin.

She blinked. Her eyelids were dry.

The other girls had fallen exhausted into bed, and their soft, sleeping breath whispered through the long room.

But something had woken her—and she had the skin-prickling sensation of being watched.

"Hello?" she whispered.

A shape moved—a shadow among shadows, like sails crossing on a black sea.

"Who's that? Stephanie?"

"I am not Stephanie," said a deep, male voice.

A man, only a few inches tall, stepped forward, his shape barely discernible against the window.

Elena recoiled, then winced at the pain in her head.

"You're—oh my God!"

"I am of the fairfolk," said Jem softly. "My dear child, your brother has sent me here to tell you that everything is going to be all right—he is doing everything he can to save you. We, the Wild Hunts-boys, are doing everything we can."

"The . . . Luka sent you?" Elena whispered. "He spoiled the offering, didn't he? I can feel the iron all around me, like I'm in a cage!"

"I understand," said Jem, brushing her hair from her face, his eyes soft and kind. "The wrath of the lore is upon you, and upon your house. Now Luka seeks to prevent the Reckoning by cladding your home in the very iron that pains you, and reversing the council's judgment. The fairfolk are a vengeful people, Elena. But I have turned my back on that. My admiration for the human spirit has grown these past two days, as I have borne witness to the selflessness and courage of your brother. I come here to prove that I am with *you*, on the side of right—on the side of decency. But also, my dear, sweet child, I come to you now because I don't know how to use a laptop."

Elena blinked. "What?"

Jem leaped onto the bed, his tiny form bending the mattress as though he was a grown man.

"Hazel has given me this driver," he said, pushing the memory stick into her hands. "And I have not the first notion of what it does."

"But I . . . my computer only has—wait, Hazel from the watchtower?"

"He now resides in your home," said Jem. "In something called a hammock."

Elena shook her head. "I don't understand."

"All that can wait," said Jem urgently. "We *must* get this . . . thing . . . into the laptop driver on the data mast."

"The data mast? But that's all the way at the top of the big hill, I can't even stand, I—"

Jem offered his arm.

"I will assist you," he said. "I am small, but I am strong. Come, we must go this instant."

Elena struggled upright with Jem pulling her hand. "But what if Little John—"

"Is Little John the large man downstairs?"

"Yes."

"He is asleep," said Jem. He thought about Little John's snores. "Very asleep," he added.

They tiptoed down the stairs, Elena wincing at the screws in the wooden banister.

"I know," said Jem. "The pain fills you, like heat. But you must keep going. Sometimes, it helps to make a fist."

He jumped up to turn the handle, and then they were outside, the wind blowing from the sea in freezing gusts, whipping Elena's hair and pressing her backward toward the abattoir.

"Take this," said Jem, unwinding a length of rope from his pack. "I will lead you. Quickly now!"

Elena gripped the rope and allowed herself to be pulled toward the path. Jem stared at the great antenna of the data mast shining silver in the distance, its lights unblinking.

"Ready?"

"I don't think so," said Elena. She lifted her head. "But I have to be, don't I?"

"Courage," said Jem approvingly. "How I love you humans."

The girl and the faerie began to climb, each footstep an agony that rang through her aching bones as her breathing, then her heart, began to slow.

45

Luka rolled through the Junkyard Knight's legs, the torches thudding behind him in a shower of sparks.

Hugo appeared from the darkness, locking his jaws around the Knight's jeans and pulling him to the ground.

The Lost Boys stood in a circle around them, smashing their bats against the floor, their masked faces staring forward.

"Get off!" shouted the Knight, kicking Hugo's legs and striking at his head.

Luka jumped on his back, tearing at the iron mask and pulling him off balance.

"Come on, Rusty," he hissed, "you're not invincible! You're not a *knight*—you're just a little boy in a big mask!"

The Junkyard Knight dropped his weapons and locked his grip on Luka's arm.

"I . . . am . . . the . . . Knight . . ." he growled. "These are my . . . followers. They . . . follow me!"

"They follow the mask," said Luka, finding the clasp with his magician's fingers. "But let's see who you are without it!"

He jumped backward, leaping away from the Junkyard Knight with the iron mask clutched in his hand.

He landed and rolled, scrambling to his feet and staring at the center of the circle where the Junkyard
Knight stood.

A thin boy stood looking at his hands. He was at least
a year younger than Luka, with a scar running over his
mouth and chin. Tears were smudging the dirt on his
face, and his breath hissed through his clenched teeth.

"You took my face," he said. "Give it back."

"No. We've got you. All of you. It's time to take off
the masks." He lifted the rake-visor from his head and
let it fall to the floor.

Rusty shook his head. "That's my face. There. You
took it. Give it back to me."

The Lost Boys' sunken, hollow eyes flickered in the
firelight.

"No," said Luka. "You need to—"

"Give it *back*!" screamed Rusty again, rushing forward and grabbing Luka around the throat, his skinny
fingers pressing into his windpipe.

Luka stared up and saw the mad darkness in the
boy's eyes. *He's going to kill me*, he realized.

He thought of his sister as his vision flickered, and
he reached out into the world to feel her pain as she
climbed with Jem.

"No," he said, his voice crushed to a whisper.

"Yes!" screamed Rusty, pressing harder, driving
Luka toward the flames, and laughing his shrill laugh
as the Huntsboy's eyes closed.

46

Elena's foot slipped. Jem caught it, pushing her back onto the ladder, the wind lashing at their faces.

"Keep going!" he said. "Only a few more steps!"

"I can't!" shouted Elena. "My hands, they're so hot on the rungs—"

"You can, and you *must*! If Luka can't deliver the Junkyard Knight to the Trenchcoats, they will arrest the Huntsboys and the fairfolk will take you as a servant!"

"What?" screamed Elena, freezing and gripping the ladder. "None of that makes—*what*? Is that what's happening to me?"

"You *must* keep going! I promise you I am telling the truth, for I cannot lie in this world without burning my skin! This is what your brother needs in order to save you, and to save himself. We must hurry, it's nearly midnight. Just a few more steps!"

Elena reached up to grab the next rung—and fell.

Jem dived after her, grabbing her by the hand and swinging her back to the ladder.

They clung there a moment, hands locked to the rungs, wind whipping against them.

"Are you all right?" said Jem after a moment.

Elena looked down, then closed her eyes.

"Yes," she hissed. "Thank you."

"Then let's—aargh!" screamed Jem, clutching his side.

"What is it?"

"My suit . . . there's a small tear . . . it's nothing, come on!"

Together, every iron-ringing step a great and terrible effort, they climbed to the mast's second story, tumbling onto the platform with lungs that felt empty and flat.

"This whole mast sings with iron," said Jem, dark blood seeping from the hole in his leather suit. "How it *burns*."

Elena nodded, looking at her hands. Her palms were scalded and pink, and she felt the whole structure grabbing at her, drawing away her strength, slowing her heartbeat.

"There it is," said Jem. "The laptop." A dark, blank screen sat exposed on the side of the platform. "What do I do? Hazel said we have to open the Goblin File and leave the rest. But I have no idea what that means!"

Elena stood, wobbling unsteadily. "All right," she said, clenching her teeth. "I can do it."

"Good," said Jem, touching her hand. He closed his eyes. "Your brother needs me—I must go to him. We will take care of everything, I swear it!"

He jumped from the side of the mast and dropped

like a stone toward the ground, aiming for a patch of shadow that sat beneath an ancient, knotted yew tree.

The shadow swallowed him without a sound, and he was gone.

Elena stood staring after him, then took an unsteady step toward the screen.

She dropped to her knees, pain screaming through her blood. "I can't . . . oh my God, I can't—"

She tried to pull herself up, but slipped. She gripped the rail again and heaved with all her strength, the flash drive outstretched, her vision fading with every breath.

She slotted the flash drive into the screen and the folder popped up immediately: she saw program files and a folder shaped like a little green goblin in the middle of photo after photo.

Photos of Hazel in the arms of a couple who could only have been his parents—he had his dad's grin and his mother's eyes—cuddling happily in a warm-looking house or laughing on the beach.

"Hazel's family," she said, sobbing as she thought of her own parents—of her mum, so far away, and her dad, gone forever.

Gritting her teeth, she double-tapped the little goblin. And fell.

47

"Any last words, *Rake*?" growled Rusty, spit dripping from his lips.

Luka's lips moved soundlessly, then, reaching into the depths of his heart and summoning all his strength, he screamed a single word:

"Jem!"

The faerie leaped from the toadstool in Luka's pocket, knocking Rusty on his back, his head striking the ground with a thud.

The Junkyard Knight lay next to his rusting iron cowl, his energy spent, his kingdom falling as the un-masking Lost Boys scattered like rats.

"Aaargh!" screamed Jem, clutching his bleeding wound as he fell into a puddle of torn metal, his skin smoking through the tear in his suit.

Luka lunged and caught him, landing on his weak leg and curling into a protective ball around the faerie.

"Did you find Elena?" he said. "Is she all right?"

"She will be," Jem managed, blood on his dark teeth. "But we need to get to your house—the Reckoning is near."

"What happened to you? Are you hurt?"

"'Tis but a scratch," said Jem, laughing. "By the lore, without my suit . . . this place . . . so much *iron*."

"Rake!" called Hazel, appearing at the top of a junk pile. "The network—it's back on! She did it!"

"Send the signal!" shouted Luka, nudging Hugo toward the door and clutching Jem to his chest. "We need to get to the house, now!"

"Done," shouted Hazel, scrambling to the ground with his laptop held aloft. "They're lit up like a Christmas tree!"

"Get Max," said Luka, relief and terror surging through him as the Reckoning loomed in his mind. "Let's go!"

Hazel propped Max's arm over his shoulder and they hobbled toward the door.

"The iron," said Jem, pointing with a weak hand. "You need to protect the house . . ."

Luka grabbed the Junkyard Knight's rusting mask and held it up to the light.

"Just another piece of scrap now," he said, tucking it under his arm as Hazel grabbed all the scrap he could carry, careful to keep it as far from Jem as possible.

Together, leaning against each other for support, the Wild Huntsboys staggered toward the door.

"I hope we've got enough," said Hazel, kicking open the door—only to find it blocked.

Clarke stared down at them, the bonfire flickering in his glasses. The driver stood behind him, chewing his gum.

"The complete wreckage of our secret plane is already being flown North," said the Trenchcoat. "Crisis averted, thanks to you boys. Good heavens," he added, striding into the church, "there's more contraband here than we could possibly have imagined."

"It's all yours," said Luka, eyes flicking past Clarke to the street beyond. Trucks were rumbling down the empty street, Wardens spilling from their doors.

Clarke nodded down at the Huntsboys. "None of you look in good shape," he said, looking at Max and Jem. "This one needs a hospital, and this one—what does he need?"

"To get back to my house," said Luka, glancing urgently at Jem. "As quickly as possible."

"Very well," said Clarke, holding up a tablet that blinked with moving lights. "We now have all their names, last known addresses, social media—everything. Very clever. We'll find them now, no matter where they run." He pointed to a red dot near the top of the screen. "Rusty's still inside, I see?"

"On the floor," said Luka. "His mask is gone. We need one more thing. My sister, Elena—she's on the Islands—"

"An evacuee," said Clarke, his voice barely audible

above the shriek of approaching sirens. "I read your file."

"She helped make this happen, and I need you to check that she's all right. That's she's happy and safe. Now, please."

Clarke, Wardens swarming around him, raised an eyebrow. "Consider it done—I'll have a helicopter dispatched within minutes."

"Thank you," said Luka, Jem clutched to his chest. "Listen, it's nearly quarter to midnight, we need to get—"

"Willoughby here will take you where you need to go," said Clarke, waving briskly at the driver. "I'll be in touch. Good luck—and thank you."

"We *are* proper spies," said Hazel as they boarded the truck. He loaded the final piece of iron into the bag. "We've got a driver and a spymaster and everything."

"I ain't *your* driver, kid," said Willoughby as they pulled away from the church. "But youse did well there, no doubt."

Luka laid the bleeding Jem on his lap. "What can we do? Is there anything we can give you?"

Jem shook his head. "Only a faerie doctor could help, and even then—" He winced, and more blood spilled from his mouth as he patted Hugo's questing nose. "This *really* hurts."

Luka held him close as the truck roared through the curfew-dark City, Willoughby throwing the big vehicle around corners and over roundabouts, running red light after red light as he chewed and swore under his breath.

"Here you are," said Willoughby, bumping onto the curb. "Good luck."

"Thanks," said Luka, as the Huntsboys spilled from the truck as it skidded onto the sidewalk outside his house, carrying each other inside with the final pieces of scrap clutched between them. Exhausted, their feet leaden, they dragged themselves into Luka's room, under Hazel's hammock, and up to the window.

"I don't think there's time for me to weld this stuff now," said Hazel. "Maybe we should just run."

"Tails, we run; heads, we stay," said Luka, plucking his coin from behind Hazel's ear. He flicked it with his thumb, and they all watched it spin through the moonlight.

"Heads," said Max, looking at the coin.

Luka turned the coin over, showing the same face etched on either side.

Max smiled ruefully.

"It's always heads," Luka said.

"You sure about this, Rake?" asked Hazel, Max leaning on his shoulder.

Luka looked down at Jem's limp form.

The faerie met his eyes and nodded.

"Yes," said Luka.

"Do it."

Hazel thrust up the window and Luka stepped out onto the roof.

He stared at the ranks of tiny faces, their black eyes shining among the saddled crows and uniformed rats, their knives clutched in pale, tight hands.

The Reckoning had begun.

48

The Gray Lady stepped forward, a sword loose in her hand.

"*Boy,*" she said. "You are too late. The house is unprotected. The lore will have its price."

Luka walked into the center of the fairfolks' circle, dragging the bag of ancient iron from the Necropolis behind him. "What about this?"

The faeries drew back from the iron's heat with an intake of breath.

"You mean to fight us?" said Doller, tongue between his teeth.

"I want nothing for myself," Luka shouted. "Only safety for my sister and care for my friends."

He opened his hand and laid Jem on the roof.

"Jem!" Esme gasped.

"Save him," said Luka. "Please. He did everything he could for me because he thought it was right. But this is my fault! I broke the pact! I know that—and it doesn't matter that I was upset or that I didn't believe in it, I *did* it. Take me, not him, and not my sister or my friends. Just me."

He turned and threw the bag off the roof, sending

the pieces of heavy iron sailing into the garden, where they clattered into the darkness.

"Rake, no!" shouted Hazel, rushing forward and leaping onto the chimney stack.

Luka held his hands at his sides. There was a shuffling of feet, and the soft noise of weapons moving in the darkness.

"I respect the lore," Luka said, as drones whirred over the City and the hum of aircraft filled the sky. Searchlights swooped through the clouds, flashing in the faeries' eyes.

Luka watched the planes for a moment—heading North.

"I accept my wrongdoing," he said. "I respect the old ways. I have no new offering to make but myself and my apology. Just save them. *Please.*"

Esme knelt at Jem's side. "He is wounded," she said. "His suit has torn. The iron is *in* him. It poisons his blood this very moment. Jem! Can you hear me?"

Jem opened his eyes.

"Esme," he said, his voice barely audible above the rumble of the planes.

"Have you any solanum in your pack?"

Jem laughed. "Only knives and meat."

Esme glanced at Luka. "Have you any in the garden?"

Luka looked bewildered. "Have I what?"

"Solanum," said Max, nodding. "Winter cherries, no? They're poisonous."

"Only to humans," said Esme.

"There's some over there," said Luka, pointing, remembering Max shooing Hugo from the red plants. "In the gardens on the edge of the park."

"The Wild Wood," whispered the Gray Lady. "Doller. Go."

Doller, his sword aloft, narrowed his eyes. "But—" he began.

"*Now*," said the Gray Lady.

"As you wish," said Doller, mounting his crow and dropping off the edge of the roof.

"I tried, mistress," said Jem. "I really did."

"Don't speak," said Esme, wiping his brow until Doller returned carrying one of the bright-red berries.

She split it in two and pressed a handful of seeds into Jem's wound. He cried out, then relaxed, the color draining from his lips.

"Will he be all right?" said Luka.

Esme pressed her hand to Jem's forehead. "Perhaps."

"The Reckoning," snapped Doller, his blade reappearing.

The Gray Lady stood and walked to where Luka hunched over Jem, lifting his chin with her sword.

"The lore," she said, "feeds on the offerings. *We* feed on them, with our bellies and our spirits. When the pacts are broken, we—"

"The lore feeds on *belief*," whispered Jem.

"I understand," said Luka, lying flat on the roof. "Take me. Please. Just don't hurt him."

"Silence!" shouted Rudge, his jowls quivering.

Hazel and Max, unable to breathe, watched their friend prostrate before this assembly of the ancient world while the sky-towers blinked under the stars.

The Gray Lady took Luka's hand in hers. "You truly care for our brother, Jem?"

"Yes," said Luka. "He's one of us now. I love him."

She thinned her lips. "And your sister—you would offer yourself in her place?"

Luka nodded. "Of course. I swore I'd keep her safe."

"Very well," said the Gray Lady. "The lore requires an offering of the offender's body. The tongue, the eyes—"

"The heart," growled Doller.

Luka closed his eyes and thought of his sister.

The Gray Lady lifted her sword and sliced through the air.

"—or the fingernails," she finished.

"What?" said Doller, Rudge, and Luka together.

Luka looked down at his hand.

The Gray Lady brushed the dirt from her dress. Clutched in her hand was a small white arc, like the blade of a tiny knife.

"My *fingernail*?" said Luka.

"A body part." The Gray Lady nodded. "We will

satisfy the lore with this morsel, and so *own* a piece of you. You have told the truth, and as is our way, we leave a gift: the *gift* of truth. From this day forth you will respect the lore; you will know our ways and you will tell *our* truths. Or there *will* be a Reckoning of blood and pain."

"What do you mean tell your truths?"

Jem sat up, chuckling as he coughed. "Now you can't lie either. Or you'll burn, just like me."

"Oh," said Luka. His head was spinning. "Thank you?"

"Good work, Rake!" shouted Hazel, laughing. He put his arm around Max's shoulders and dribbled coffee on his tongue.

Esme helped Jem to his feet.

"You realize you're stuck here, don't you?" she said. "You chose the humans over the lore. You cannot come back."

He nodded, a hand clutching his side. "This is where I *belong*, Esme. It's like the boy said: I'm one of them now."

Esme nodded stiffly, then bowed and kissed his hand.

"Keep an eye on them," she said, a tear at the corner of her eye. "We'll be watching."

Jem gave her a quick hug, then climbed onto Luka's shoulders as the fairfolk leaped into the sky, the rats of the Elder Guard swinging from the crows' feet.

Hazel and Max fell onto the roof beside Luka and Jem. Hugo scrambled through the window, nosing his way into the pile of bodies and licking their faces as the faeries vanished into the blanket of stars.

"Thank you," said Luka when they were alone again. "All of you."

They sat quietly together as the night paled toward morning and the world—its trees and spires kissed with sunlit dew—began a bright new day.

49

Elena opened her eyes.

The pull from the metal beneath her had gone, and she felt restored. She felt strong and light.

She made fists, then relaxed her grip and smiled. "Luka! Oh, what have you done *now*?"

Approaching the edge of the mast's platform, she looked at the ground, a hundred feet down a wet and rickety ladder.

"Let's try another way," she said. And jumped.

Ellie fell, her clothes zipping behind her in the wind, before landing like a cat and running, running faster than she'd ever thought possible, a new strength flowing through her from the wind and the sky and the earth. A strength she knew exactly how to use, she thought, turning toward the dormitory of sleeping girls, and the abattoir that rang with the cries of caged and frightened animals.

50

"Try this one," said Hazel, sitting cross-legged on Luka's gamer chair. "Two plus two is five."

Luka took another slurp of tea and narrowed his eyes against the morning sun. He looked at the others, smiling through their cuts and scrapes.

"Do I have to?"

"Yes," said Max, nodding. He was holding a bag of frozen peas to his swollen eye and buttering toast with his free hand.

"Two plus two is . . ." started Luka, feeling the heat start on his skin like a palm held over a candle. "Fi—I can't do it!

"Hurts, doesn't it?" said Jem, shuddering. "Imagine what it's like telling a really *big* lie."

"So, I can't even get things wrong at school? What if I genuinely don't know the answer?"

"Oh, you won't burn for stupidity, don't worry." Jem chuckled.

"Big relief for you, numbnuts," said Hazel, completing another mission on *Final Crisis IV*. "This is so *easy*, I don't get what people see in this at all."

"Most people haven't launched a real-life campaign against the fairfolk and a bunch of masked vigilante kids," said Max. "And most people dilute their coffee. You know, with hot water."

"Idiots," said Hazel, his teeth stained and brown.

"Hang on," said Luka, reaching over and appearing a crust of bread from behind Max's ear. "Ow! Come *on*—I can't even do *tricks* without burning?"

"Tricks are just little lies, Rake," said Hazel. He turned to Jem. "How's your roof tile?"

"Perfect, thank you. There's even a slug on this one. A real treat."

Hazel wrinkled his nose. "I left that there as a joke."

"Good one," said Jem, slurping the slug like spaghetti.

"You get a text from your sister?" said Max.

Luka nodded, then took another slice of toast. "She's fine. Felt better the second the Gray Lady cut my fingernail. *Much* better, apparently. Said she'll explain when she's home for her visit next month."

"She's lucky," said Jem. "Lucky to have a brother like you."

Luka screwed up his face. "I don't know about that. It was me who got her into that mess."

"And you who got her out," said Hazel.

Luka shook his head. "I didn't do it alone. It was all of us. We're a team."

"That reminds me," said Hazel, typing quickly into his phone.

Luka and Max felt their phones respond.

Brains has changed the name of
this chat . . .

"'The Wild Huntsboys,'" Luka read aloud. "Nice."

Another phone beeped.

"Whose is that?" said Hazel.

"It's coming from your pocket," said Luka, standing and crossing the room.

Hazel patted his boilersuit, then stood and produced a thin, white handset, its screen flashing with a new message. "This is not mine! Even I've never seen tech like this!"

"Open it," said Max.

Hazel handed the phone to Luka. "You do it. I don't even want to be near that thing."

Luka turned the phone in his hand. It looked almost like a bar of soap—perfectly smooth, almost soft.

"What kind of phone is this?" he said, running his hand over the screen, which immediately lit up. "And how does it already have my fingerprint installed?"

Hazel's eyes flashed. "Oooh," he said. "I know whose phone this is!"

"What does the message say?" asked Jem.

Luka thumbed it open.

"'Pull the tail,'" he read.

The phone started ringing.

Luka looked at the others, then swiped to answer and put it on speakerphone. "Hello?"

"Good morning," said Clarke. "I trust you've heard from Elena. Quite the scene when our chopper arrived, I'm told. She and the other girls have been moved, of course: the abattoir had been mysteriously destroyed. You wouldn't know anything about that, would you?"

Luka glanced at Jem, who shrugged.

"No," he said carefully.

"Hmmm. Someone had set all the animals free *and* hung the foreman from a lamppost by his underpants. Most unusual. Anyway, I was discussing your particular case with my superiors, and we have some other small problems that rather suit your particular skills and . . . connections. Are you ready?"

Luka held his friends' eyes—then nodded.

"Yes," he said. "We are."

"Good," said Clarke. "Pull the tail, then. One hour." The line went dead.

Hugo ran in a circle, Jem clinging to his collar. Hazel leaped onto Luka's desk and ruffled Max's hair. "I knew it!" he shouted. "I *knew* it!"

Luka smiled. "Huntsboys," he said. "Let's hunt."

Acknowledgments

I loved writing this story. The process was very different this time: starting with the original ideas—at first, little more than a jumble of loose threads without an obvious connection—and ending with writing the final drafts in lockdown. As ever, my work was supported by a host of wonderful people.

Thank you to my editor at Viking, Maggie Rosenthal. You saw the angel in the marble right from the start and helped me find the Huntsboys' truest form with patience and clarity. I sincerely appreciate your vision and guidance. Thank you to my agent, Molly Ker Hawn, for keeping this train running, and for your support and advice. Thank you to Ken Wright, my publisher, for supporting me in another creative endeavor, and to my copyeditors and proofreaders, Marinda Valenti and Abigail Powers, for catching and correcting my many errors. Thank you to my cover artist, Owen Richardson—your fantastic artwork has brought these characters to life and immortalized my dog, the real Hugo the Weimaraner, beautifully.

Thank you to Nnamdi Obi for consulting on Hazel's hair, and to George Dufty for your insightful reading. Thank you to the Hutchison boys, Colin and Neil, for giving the story its first-ever bedtime reading—and its first fan art! Thank you to my family and my friends (Paul Dickov?) for your network of support. Thank you to my grandparents, Ellice and Jim, whose stories of wartime Glasgow and evacuation to the islands filled my imagination and breathed life into the Huntsboys' world.

Thank you to my wee bears, Tessie and Milo. You fill me with happiness and make me proud every day. I love you both with all my heart.

Most importantly, thank you to my wife, Julie. You see things in my writing that I just can't see myself, and—here it is in print—every time you've suggested a major change, *you've been right*. This time you thought I should change the title, which pulled the last thread into place and made the Huntsboys complete. My darling, your support, wisdom, and love are so essential to the production of my work that your name should be on the cover. I love you.